A TIME TO REJOICE
A CHRISTIAN ROMANCE

JULIETTE DUNCAN

A TIME FOR EVERYTHING SERIES - BOOK 4

Cover Design by http://www.StunningBookCovers.com

Copyright © 2019 Juliette Duncan
All rights reserved.

"A Time to Rejoice" is a work of fiction. Names, characters, and incidents are all products of the author's imagination or are used for fictional purposes. Any mentioned brand names, places, and trade marks remain the property of their respective owners, bear no association with the the author, and are used for fictional purposes only.

THE HOLY BIBLE, NEW INTERNATIONAL VERSION®, NIV® Copyright © 1973, 1978, 1984, 2011 by Biblica, Inc.™ Used by permission. All rights reserved worldwide.

PRAISE FOR "A TIME TO REJOICE"

"This story is truly a story of redemption and unconditional love. A great feel good story! I highly recommend you read the entire series but this was my favorite. I am going to miss Bruce and Wendy and their clan. " ~ JLS

"What a beautiful story of family love and perseverance. God works so wonderfully through this family and is faithful to all of us no matter our sin. I have enjoyed this series immensely and feel this wraps up Bruce and Wendy's blended family nicely ~Linda L

"It's always sad when a series I love comes to an end. Juliette isn't afraid to go into the sinful or tragic parts of life. The redeeming grace of Jesus is always presented in her stories as her characters go through the trials and tribulations of daily life." ~Jan

"What a remarkable finale to a great Christian series! A series of heartache, loss, shocking revelations, and intrigue capture the reader's heart, but with faith in God's love, healing and blessings, the situations result in a beautiful ending!" ~Jana

FOREWORD

HELLO! Thank you for choosing to read this book - I hope you enjoy it! Please note that this story is told from two different points of view – Wendy, an Australian, and Bruce, a cowboy from Texas. Australian spelling and terminology have been used when in Wendy's point of view – they're not typos!

As a thank you for reading this book, I'd like to offer you a FREE GIFT. That's right - my FREE novella, "Hank and Sarah - A Love Story" is available exclusively to my newsletter subscribers. Go to http://www.julietteduncan.com/subscribe to get the ebook for FREE, and to be notified of future releases.

I hope you enjoy both books! Have a wonderful day!

Juliette

FOREWORD

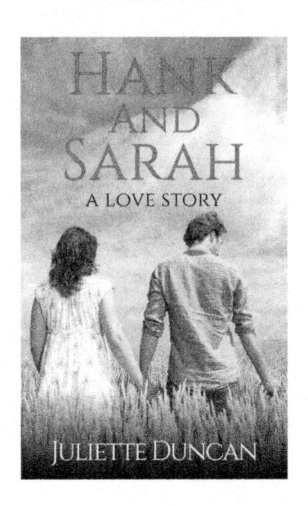

PROLOGUE

"There is a time for everything,
and a season for every activity under the heavens:
a time to be born and a time to die,
a time to plant and a time to uproot,
a time to kill and a time to heal,
a time to tear down and a time to build,
a time to weep and a time to laugh,
a time to mourn and a time to dance,
a time to scatter stones and a time to gather them,
a time to embrace and a time to refrain from embracing,
a time to search and a time to give up,
a time to keep and a time to throw away,
a time to tear and a time to mend,
a time to be silent and a time to speak,
a time to love and a time to hate,
a time for war and a time for peace."

Ecclesiastes 3:1-8

CHAPTER 1

Granbury, Texas

How had his life become so pathetic? The self-pitying thought was just one of many that had coursed through Andrew McCarthy's mind for the last three hours as he'd sat at the bar nursing whiskey after whiskey, feeling sorry for himself. Everywhere around him the world moved faster, people going about their everyday lives, but his just seemed to be standing still. It felt like he was running in quicksand and no matter how hard he tried, he couldn't keep his head above the sand. He wondered why he even bothered to try anymore.

Would anyone notice? Would anyone even care if he simply disappeared? He somehow doubted it. He was only dragging everyone down. He was a hopeless good-for-nothing and a drunk. A druggie, if he really wanted to be honest. But most days he refused to acknowledge his affliction, even though just a few short hours ago he'd snorted a line of coke to help him get through the day. He'd been hungover and struggling to get through the morning chores, so he used just a little to give himself a small pick-me-up.

If Nate noticed something was up, he didn't say anything. Andrew had convinced himself there was nothing wrong with using a little. He wasn't an abuser; he could stop when he wanted to. Besides, it wasn't any different than people who drank those 5-hour energy drinks to stay awake. They were full of stimulants. This wasn't any different.

He hadn't always needed drugs and alcohol to help him through the day, but ever since the accident, he needed something to numb the pain. Memories of the wreck flashed before him, and he took a long pull of his drink. The whiskey burned his throat, but Andrew welcomed the familiar heat. Images of the mangled truck still haunted him more than ten years later. The image of his mother lying broken and unmoving haunted him even more. Knowing it was his fault weighed him down with guilt and shame.

The officer had told his father he hadn't been speeding, but Andrew knew he'd taken the dangerous curve too fast. His mother had even warned him to slow down as he came up to it, but like usual, he didn't listen. He'd always lived life in the fast lane, never heeding other's warnings and his mother had paid the ultimate price.

In the weeks and months after the funeral, he'd been angry and defensive, refusing to accept even the littlest responsibility for his actions. But no amount of excuses could bring his mother back. He could tell his dad, Bruce, blamed him. So did his twin, Nate. That had cut deep; the bond between twins was supposed to be unbreakable, but that fateful day had been a wedge that had torn the boys apart. That break had continued to separate over the years until it felt like a chasm that could never be mended.

His father and his younger brother Aiden had eventually come to terms with his mom's death and slowly begun trying to mend fences with him. Nate, not so much. It had been a bumpy road, but things were almost cordial now since he'd eaten humble pie and asked for a job at the family ranch. However, Andrew still felt some distance with his dad, although the old man had tried reaching out to him many times over the years. Andrew just couldn't get past the guilt of being responsible for his mom's death and leaving his dad on his own.

It was more difficult now that his dad had remarried and moved to Australia. He'd met his new wife on a trip to Ireland. Apparently, the widow and widower had hit it off and traveled together across Europe before becoming engaged. It all seemed sudden to Andrew. Wendy seemed a nice enough woman, but he couldn't handle his dad moving on from Mom. Maybe it was because Andrew had never moved past her death.

He went to take a sip from his glass, but his depth perception was off. It must have been the low lights and the foggy atmosphere of the bar that caused him to drop it. At least that's what he told himself as the glass slipped from his fingers and the last bit of amber liquid spilled onto the bar. A four-letter word flew from his mouth as he tried to mop it up with some napkins, but his hands wouldn't cooperate, and he managed to make even more of a mess.

"Here, I've got it." The bartender was already there with a wet bar towel and made quick work of soaking up the spill.

"Sorry, Tom. Guess it's a little darker in here than usual." The excuse sounded feeble even to his ears. "Do you mind pouring me another since I spilled that one?"

"How about I pour you a coffee instead?" Tom offered as he took Andrew's glass and set it in the sink with a clink. He grabbed a ceramic mug from behind the counter and poured a steaming cup from the pot. "Here, on the house."

Andrew scowled as Tom placed the mug in front of him. "It'd be better if it had a shot of whiskey in it. How about you hook me up?"

Tom sighed visibly. "I think you've had enough for tonight, Andrew. Drink your coffee. It will help you sober up some. I'll call you a cab in a little bit, or I can call Nate and see if he'll swing by."

A rush of heat flamed up Andrew's neck to the tips of his ears as he flushed with embarrassment. A few of the patrons seated at the bar near him studiously avoided looking at him, but he knew they'd heard. He'd come into the Double Deuce looking to relax and have a drink or two, not to be hassled. He got enough of that at the ranch.

He stumbled off the bar stool and pulled out some wadded-up bills and tossed them on the bar. "Thanks for nothing," he mumbled as he made his way outside. Tom called after him, but Andrew ignored him as he stumbled into the warm summer night.

He looked down Main Street trying to decide which way to go. South would take him back to the ranch, but it was almost ten miles and too far to walk in his condition. He'd been dropped off in town by Darby, one of the ranch hands on his way to Fort Worth. He wouldn't be back until Sunday, so getting a ride back with him wasn't an option. He could call his brother for a ride, but the last thing Andrew needed was a lecture from Nate about his drinking.

So, he headed north to work off some of his frustration. He'd figure out how to get home in a bit. Right now, he just wanted to get away. Away from everything. Everyone was always trying to tell him what to do or hassle him over how he chose to live his life. He'd been on his own for a while now, so he didn't need anybody's help. He would decide when enough was enough.

He didn't know how long he walked. He let his anger carry him until it turned into despair. For the second time that night he wondered how his life had gotten so pathetic. Anguish gripped his heart and laid like an iron anchor in his chest.

Whenever you feel unloved, unimportant, or insecure, remember to Whom you belong.

Andrew stopped in his tracks and shook his fists at the sky. *No! I belong to no one. You made that clear ten years ago when You took my mother from me and made my family hate me.* Inside he railed at the God he had left behind over a decade ago. A God who had abandoned him.

I will never leave you or forsake you.

When you pass through the waters, I will be with you; And through the rivers, they shall not overflow you. When you walk through the fire, you shall not be burned, Nor shall the flame scorch you.

Andrew began to walk again, this time much faster as if he could outrun the words of the Lord. Tears stung his eyes, and his chest heaved with emotion. He wasn't about to listen to a

God that hadn't been there for him, who hadn't protected him when he needed Him most.

The Lord will fight for you, you need only be still.

He kicked a rock in frustration. Not this time. Never again. Andrew vowed to walk away from the Lord the way He had walked away from him. After another mile, he saw the flashing neon sign at Delia's, and his stomach rumbled, reminding him that he hadn't eaten anything since lunch.

They were open all night. Perfect.

CHAPTER 2

It had been a long day, and it looked like it was going to be an even longer night. Mary Alice, the new waitress, had called in sick again, and Delia had asked Melody if she could pull a double to cover for her. She'd been here since five a.m., and all she wanted to do was go home and get off her feet, but she couldn't pass up the opportunity for the overtime. Not since her mother, Nancy, had spent all her social security money on booze, part of which was supposed to help Melody cover rent and groceries.

With a resigned sigh, Melody readily agreed to help Delia out. Her daughter was staying over at their neighbor's house, so she didn't have to worry about a babysitter, and it wasn't like she really had a choice. *If a man does not work, he should not eat.* Wasn't that the saying?

She felt like she'd done nothing but work since she was sixteen, but she didn't really have a choice. When her father left, her mom fell apart and turned to alcohol. Many nights she didn't even come home, and when she did, she was wasted and passed out for hours on end. Melody did the best she could to get herself ready for school and scrounged around for what little food she could find. But when they'd been evicted from the house and were sleeping in the car, she'd decided she had to get a job.

Walking into Delia's after school one day, she begged for one. She'd do anything. Delia had been reluctant at first, but Melody was persistent. By the end of the evening shift, she'd worn her down and started as a dishwasher the very next day. It was hard work and long hours after school, but it was enough money for her and her mom to get off the street and into a small one-bedroom trailer. Melody let her mother have the bedroom while she slept on the couch.

Delia had taken a shine to Melody once she saw her work ethic and her dedication. Delia had also been a stickler about her education, not having gotten past the eighth grade herself. She gave Melody longer breaks when the restaurant was slow in order for her to get her homework done so she wouldn't get behind in school. She even baked her a special cake and gave her a one hundred dollar bonus the day she graduated. It had been a bittersweet moment, as Melody's own mother had been too drunk to attend her graduation ceremony. But Delia had always been like a second mom to her and stepped in where it counted. The woman had given her a chance when no one else would, and she would forever be grateful.

Melody had worked her way up from dishwasher to hostess, and now to head waitress. Sometimes she even ran the restaurant when Delia took a vacation, which wasn't often. But it felt good knowing that Delia trusted her enough to be responsible for the place long enough for her to step away for a long weekend to go visit her grandson in Abilene or down to the coast for some saltwater fishing. Oh, how Melody wished she could take a vacation, even a tiny one.

But thoughts of time off were pushed to the side as the dinner rush began to start up. She had customers to serve. They had the main dinner rush between six and eight, and then it slowed down just enough for them to clean up and regroup before another late-night dinner rush from ten-thirty to eleven-thirty when the Carmine Metal factory's second shift let out at ten o'clock. It was only about six miles from the diner, and Delia's probably saw about forty to fifty of the workers every night.

Melody didn't mind the rush because it kept her busy. If she didn't keep moving when pulling a double, she'd be asleep on her feet. Even though she was exhausted once the last few stragglers left, her apron was heavy with the generous tips they left her, and her heart was filled with joy and love from the lively conversations. A lot of the people were old-timers and had been punching a clock since before she'd worked there. She'd grown up in front of many of them, and now they were watching her daughter grow up too. They were all like extended family. She didn't know what she would have done without the love and support of Delia, her staff, and her customers.

She'd just finished stacking the last rack of dishes in the washer when the overhead bell tinkled. Melody checked the clock on the wall. Just after one-thirty a.m. They didn't get too many people in at this time. Curiosity got the best of her and she poked her head through the swinging kitchen doors. It was a single person, a man who looked a little worse for wear. Melody recognized him, as he'd been in every now and then, but she couldn't remember his name. She knew he worked at the Cedar Springs Ranch and Resort on the outskirts of town. Normally, he came in with a group of ranch hands, but tonight he was alone. She couldn't remember a time when he'd ever come in by himself, or anywhere near this late.

She frowned at his disheveled state. As he waited to be seated, he swayed a bit on his feet as if he wasn't quite steady. At one point he even had to balance on the hostess podium. She'd seen the signs before and knew he was drunk. She had her suspicions confirmed when she grabbed a menu and walked up to greet him. The smell of sweat and alcohol permeated the air and made her stomach roll. She wasn't too keen on dealing with a drunk, but he seemed relatively harmless at the moment.

He'd tried to plaster a smile on his face when she greeted him, and even though his "How ya doin'?" was slurred and came out more like "Hawww, y donnn", he wasn't belligerent.

Replying with her own fake smile on her face, she greeted him warmly. "I'm fine. Thanks for asking. Table for one?"

"Yup." He hiccupped as he answered, and another wave of alcohol hit her. Trying not to grimace, she asked him to follow her.

She bypassed the tables since she didn't think he'd be able to stay upright in a chair. She briefly considered sitting him at the counter where she could keep a better eye on him, but the bar stools had no backs, and that was just asking for trouble. She finally settled on a booth in the corner out of the way. He made his way precariously to the table, only managing to bump into one table before he flopped into the booth. Melody had to stop herself from reaching out to steady him. He managed to right himself well enough on his own.

"I'll grab you a cup of coffee while you decide on what you want." He didn't even respond as she went to the back. Delia had begun a fresh pot and it was only another minute before it was done. Melody poured him a steaming mug of coffee, straight black. He looked like he needed it.

She set the mug in front of him and pulled out her pad.

He grabbed it gratefully, cupping the warm mug between his hands as he closed his eyes and let his head droop a little.

"What can I get you?" she said a little loudly, not wanting him to pass out at the table. A scalding cup of coffee in his hands was an accident waiting to happen.

He opened his eyes with a start and looked up at her as if just noticing she was there. It took a minute for his eyes to focus and then he said, "I'll have two eggs over hard, hash browns extra crispy, with bacon and wheat toast. Please."

She raised an eyebrow at his manners, not quite expecting them in his current state. "Coming right up."

She put the order in to Tom and went about her night duties of refilling the salt, pepper, and sugar shakers as well as the ketchup bottles. Every now and then she would glance over at the guy in the booth to make sure he was okay, but so far, he seemed to be nursing his cup of coffee and staying awake.

Tom had the order ready in no time, and Melody took it out to the table. She set the plate of food in front of him and asked if he needed anything else.

"Just some Tabasco for my hash browns if you have some."

"We have some bottles at the counter, I'll grab you one."

"Thanks," he mumbled through a mouthful of food. He ate with gusto, like a man who hadn't had a good meal in a while. Judging by the gauntness of his face, maybe he hadn't. But, Melody wasn't one to judge.

He who is without sin can cast the first stone.

She had more than enough skeletons in her closet that she didn't try to pretend to walk in other people's shoes.

She grabbed a bottle of Tabasco quickly and the coffee pot. Setting the bottle on the table, she topped up his coffee and left him a couple of extra napkins.

"I have to do some cleanup in back. It'll take me a few minutes, so just holler if you need anything else." Normally, she wouldn't leave a customer by themselves for more than a minute or two, but she had closing duties to complete, and he was busy stuffing his face anyway. Honestly, she didn't think he'd even heard her until he grunted and nodded his head in her direction as she turned to leave.

She went through her closing routine, even though they technically were open twenty-four hours a day and didn't actually close. But they still had duties that needed to be done before the morning rush, like changing out the fryer oil, finishing the dishes, wrapping silverware, and taking the trash out. She tried to hurry through her routine, but it was probably twenty or thirty minutes before she was done with everything. She'd checked on the man once in between cleaning, but had left him alone for about fifteen minutes.

Fretting, she hustled out of the kitchen into the diner and stopped in her tracks. His plate was clear and pushed off to the side. His head was down on his arms. She walked toward him hesitantly, not wanting to startle him. As she got closer, she heard soft snores coming from the table. Reaching it, she started collecting the dishes. She might have let the silverware rattle off the plates a little louder than was necessary, but it was to no avail. He didn't so much as twitch. He was out cold.

She groaned. What was she supposed to do? She looked around the restaurant. The dining area was empty. Tom was busy in back prepping food for the morning, and Delia had gone home for a bit to rest until she came back at three-thirty to relieve Melody. He wasn't hurting anybody. Maybe it wouldn't hurt to let him sleep a little longer.

She went about her business clearing off his table and mopping the floors. With the lull, she had time to help Tom prep the food for breakfast and then restock the shelves from the stock room. About an hour later, the doorbell tinkled again. Melody looked up from the counter, surprised that it was Delia.

"What's that look for?" Delia teased. "When the cat's away, the mice will play?"

Melody chuckled. "No, it's not that. I was just wondering who was coming in at this time. Normally, you come through the back."

"I forgot my keycard and didn't feel like knocking in case Tom was in the freezer or stock room and didn't hear me." As she made her way to the counter, her gaze fell on the man dozing in the corner. She eyed Melody with an arched brow. "Who's that? And why is he sleeping in my diner?"

Sheepishly, Melody replied, "He came in a little bit ago. He was drunk and—"

"This isn't a halfway house, Melody," Delia cut in.

Holding her hands up, Melody apologized. "I know. He

came in and ordered and then ate. Had a few cups of coffee to sober up. He fell asleep when I was out back changing the fry oil and I didn't have the heart to wake him."

"Has he paid?"

"Um…" Melody felt her face turn red. "Not yet."

Delia's eyes hardened. "We don't feed strays for free."

"I know he's good for it. He's one of the hands at Cedar Springs Ranch and Resort. I think he's one of the sons. He'll be good for it." Melody wrung her hands hoping Delia wouldn't take the meal out of her pay. The meal didn't cost much, but every penny counted right now.

Delia took her time answering but finally sighed in defeat. Pointing a finger at Melody she said, "Fine, but don't make me regret it. He doesn't pay, you will." As an afterthought, she waved her hand at him. "But, he's got to go. Wake him up and send him on his way."

With that dismissal, she headed into the back muttering about charity cases and bleeding hearts. Melody smiled to herself. Even though Delia came across hard-nosed, she had a soft spot a mile wide. You just had to get past the rough exterior to find it.

Melody gathered her tips for the night, collected her purse, and made her way over to the snoozing man. But how was she to wake him? She tried whispering 'Hey' a few times, each one a little louder, but that didn't work. She was reluctant to get close to him in case he was the type to jump and lash out when startled. So, she did the next best thing and nudged him in the arm with a menu. Nothing. *Great.*

Finally, she did the only thing she could think of and clapped her hands three times and yelled 'Hey' again, this time as loud as she could. That worked. He jerked awake thumping his knees sharply on the booth table.

"Oh good, you're awake!" she said, her voice oozing sweetness. "Here's your ticket. You can pay me here." She tried to keep her face neutral and innocent, but on the inside, she wanted to laugh at his wry expression. He probably believed she meant for him to hurt himself.

He fished around in his pocket for his wallet and tossed a couple of twenties on the table.

"Oh, that's way too much."

He shook his head. "Keep it. Consider it table rent for the nap."

His eyes were still blurry and bloodshot, but her heart melted a little when he flashed her a quick grin. He had the same dimples as his brother who came in from time to time. Underneath the haggard face and dark circles under his eyes, he was a rather attractive man. But that wasn't something Melody really wanted to consider. She hadn't dated anyone in almost five years. Not since Jason had run off with her best friend when he found out she was pregnant with Jasmine. She didn't need any distractions while she tried to take care of her mother and raise her daughter.

He slid out of the booth and stumbled to his feet. She wanted to ask him if he was sure he was okay, but she knew Delia wanted him gone, so she kept silent as he made his way to the door. Her heart was heavy as the doorbell tinkled one last time before the door closed behind him. She watched him walk past the front window and then he was gone into the night.

"You can head on out if you want to."

Melody jumped at the sound of Delia's voice behind her. She hadn't realized she'd been staring off into space once the man had left.

"Um...thanks," Melody said, pulled from her thoughts. She grabbed her purse and keys and headed out the back door. She headed around the front and had just started the walk home when she noticed something huddled against the dumpster on the side of the diner. Blinking in the darkness, her eyes adjusted and she saw it was him.

Torn between walking away and helping, words from the Bible she'd heard recently played in her mind. *Share with the Lord's people who are in need. Practice hospitality.* Her steps wavered. She normally wouldn't ask a strange man into her home, but she felt the Lord's will on her heart guiding her to be kind and assuring her that it would be okay. Her feet moved on their own volition and carried her toward the man on the ground.

He didn't look up when she stopped in front of him. His eyes were closed again, so she reached out and shook his shoulder, once, twice before he finally opened them and blinked. "Hey, wake up. You can't sleep here."

He groaned and pulled his arms tighter around his body. "Come on, please. I'm not hurting anyone. I'll be gone in the morning." His voice was slurred, either with alcohol or sleep or both. But she could hear the frustration in his voice.

"Come on, I've got a couch you can rest on. It'll be a lot more comfortable than the dumpster."

That got his attention. His head shot up and his brows lifted. "You're offering me a place to crash?"

"Just for a few hours." Her bravado began to waver. "You don't have drugs on you or anything like that, do you?"

He took a moment to answer, and her heart thudded in her chest. "No, I'm clean."

She expelled the breath she'd been holding. "All right, well come on then. It's late, and I'm tired. It's only about a half-mile walk."

She didn't wait to see if he was following or not. She just turned around and started walking, hearing the scuffle of gravel behind her as he scrambled to his feet. He was tall and his long legs caught up to her short stride almost immediately. He walked beside her on the side nearest the road, as if to protect her from oncoming cars. Not that there would be any traffic at this time of night.

They walked in companionable silence, the sounds of the frogs and the cicadas the only noise. Despite the late hour, she loved this time of night. There was a certain peace in the stillness, and the stars were exceptionally bright since they weren't obscured by harsh big city lights. She liked her small town. She felt safe and comfortable in it.

"This is me," she finally said when they reached the dirt lane that led to her tiny two-bedroom house. It was small, but it worked for her and Jasmine and her mom Nancy. The house was dark, which meant her mom wasn't home, which was good. She didn't feel like dealing with her mother tonight or explaining why there was a strange man there.

Again she was struck by his manners as he held the screen door open for her while she unlocked the front door. She switched on the front room light and tossed her keys on the counter. He stood just inside the door, looking slightly unsure of what to do.

She pointed to the couch. "Sleep there. I'll grab you some blankets and a pillow." She pointed down the hall. "Bathroom is there, kitchen there. If you get thirsty, glasses are above the sink."

He nodded and watched her as she grabbed the spare blankets from the linen closet. She didn't have any extra pillows, so she ducked into her room and grabbed Jasmine's Cinderella pillow. She wouldn't need it tonight, and Melody could wash it before she needed it the following night.

When she handed him the blankets and pillow, he accepted the Cinderella pillow and smiled. She saw the flash of dimples again and felt a twinge of butterflies in her belly.

"Thanks again. Much obliged for your hospitality. I'm Andrew, by the way."

"Melody. And it's no trouble." She turned and walked down the hall, but stopped. Looking over her shoulder, she warned him, "And for the record, I keep a *45* next to my bed." She didn't know what made her say that.

He dipped his head. "Understood. And I won't be any trouble. Just mean to get a bit of shut-eye and then I'll be on my way."

It was her turn to nod her head silently, then she left him alone and walked to her room, shutting the door behind her. She leaned against it for a minute as she felt her cheeks warm. The man had a strange effect on her, and she wasn't sure how she felt about it. Good thing he'd be gone tomorrow.

She stood at the door for a few minutes longer just listening. She heard the sound of shoes hitting the floor and then the familiar creak of the couch as he settled in for the night. A minute later, the light in the front room clicked off, and it was quiet.

Melody crawled into bed, checking to make sure her gun was secure at her bedside. She hadn't been joking when she told him she was armed. She said her nightly prayer thanking God for His blessings and asking Him to keep her and her family safe, adding the stranger on the couch for good measure, too. In no time at all, she was fast asleep.

CHAPTER 3

Morning came much too soon. Andrew felt like it had only been mere minutes since he laid down, instead of the hours that had actually passed. As his mind slowly woke up, he became very aware of the hammer that was savagely pounding in his head. He stayed where he was for a moment without opening his eyes, willing the sharp pains to ease. As he lay there, a feeling of unease crept over him causing the hair on his arms to stand up. It was the feeling of being watched.

Not wanting to make any sudden movements, he slowly opened one eye. His vision was blurry, but he didn't immediately recognize his surroundings. He wasn't in the bunkhouse, and he wasn't in his old bed either. In fact, it looked like he was on the couch in a small room. All he could see was a tiny person standing in front of him. He blinked the sleep from his eyes and opened them again. The tiny person was still there, only now she was staring at him with her head cocked to the side, hazel eyes wide and curious.

The little girl couldn't have been more than four or five with shoulder length blonde hair that looked tangled from sleep. She wore cartoon pajamas and had a worn stuffed rabbit tucked under her arm. It was missing an eye and looked like it hadn't been washed in a while. Before he had a chance to say anything, the little girl spoke first.

"Why are you using my pillow?"

"Huh?" The question threw him completely off guard.

"My pillow." She pointed by his head. "Why do you have my pillow?"

Automatically, he turned to see where she was pointing. The cartoon pillow. That's what she was after.

"I was just borrowing it. Would you like it back?" He held it out.

She stood there watching him. As silence ticked on, he wasn't sure what to do. He shook the pillow at her again, offering it with a small smile, but she still didn't move. Frowning, he pulled it back.

She shuffled her feet before she spoke again. "I'm not supposed to take anything from strangers. Mom's rules."

He glanced toward the back bedroom, but it was still dark. He looked back at the little girl and nodded sagely. "That's good advice. Your mom is a smart person. Why don't I toss it over on the chair and then you can get it when you're ready? That way you aren't taking anything from me."

She cocked her little head to the other side as she regarded his suggestion. After a minute she nodded and said, "Okay" in a sing-song little voice.

Very gently he tossed the pillow onto the chair opposite. He made sure to scoot to the far end of the couch and stay seated while she retrieved the pillow. Once she got it, much to his chagrin, she turned and sat down with it in her lap. He'd hoped she would take it and go back to her room or wherever she'd appeared from. He wasn't good at making small talk with little kids sober, let alone fighting the mother of all hangovers.

Suddenly, she started to chatter about anything and everything. The rabbit's name was Mr. Wigglesworth, and her name was Jasmine. She was five and a half. That half was obviously significant, because she mentioned it three times. By the time she was telling him the names of the kids in her class and those who still wet the bed, he heard the back bedroom door open with a slam. The noise clattered through his head like a freight train, causing him to wince.

"Jasmine!" her mom called sharply. "What are you doing here? You're supposed to be at Mrs. Bailey's house." The woman, he couldn't remember her name, looked disheveled, her long dark hair wild from sleep. She wore striped pajama pants and a Houston Astros t-shirt. Under normal circumstances, Andrew would have thought she looked cute, but right now his head was pounding too hard for him to care. He even struggled to remember how he'd ended up in her house.

"She got ah 'mergency' and had to bring me home early. It's otay, I used my key," Jasmine said proudly.

Andrew grinned as the kid struggled with her words. She really was all kinds of adorable. But, apparently, her mother was not amused. She had one hand on her hip and looked ready to strangle someone. But her anger was interrupted.

"Who's that?"

The question caught both the adults off guard, and their gazes darted toward each other and then they looked away just as quickly.

"He's uh...a friend of the family. But, he was just leaving." The woman's hazel eyes implored Andrew to make haste. Catching his cue, he began searching for his shoes.

"But, why is he leaving now?" Apparently, Jasmine's curiosity and inquisitiveness weren't to be denied.

"Because he has to go to work, and so do I," her mom explained.

Andrew found his shoes under the couch and tied them quickly. But not quickly enough.

"Where do you work?" Curious hazel eyes stared back at him, the questions in them endless.

He wasn't sure how much he should reveal, but he figured honesty was the best policy. "I'm a ranch hand at Cedar Springs Ranch."

"What's a wanch hand?"

Andrew couldn't help but laugh, in spite of his headache. "I work on a farm and take care of the animals."

Before the little girl could ask another question, her mother interceded. "Now, Jasmine, that's enough questions. Why don't you take your pillow and Mr. Wigglesworth and climb in my bed and watch cartoons?"

She looked like she might protest, but when her mother raised one brow and narrowed her eyes like only moms can do, the little girl left without protest, though her footsteps may have been a little heavier than necessary. The woman in front of him sighed in relief when the door finally closed behind her. Looking at Andrew, she apologized. "I'm sorry she bothered you. She wasn't supposed to be here until noon."

"It was no bother. She's a cute kid." They both stood there awkwardly, both looking everywhere except at the other. Not wanting to make things more awkward, he headed for the door. "I'd better get going. Thanks again for the couch. I really appreciate it. Sorry, I can't remember your name."

She pinned him with a narrow gaze as she told him it was Melody. After she closed the door behind him, he walked to the end of her driveway. Turning to glance at the house before heading down the road, he saw her watching from behind the curtains before they snapped shut. A small grin grew on his face.

By the time he turned down the dusty road and walked under the giant wooden arch that marked the resort property, Andrew was more than two hours late for morning chores. He'd tried to hitch a ride to get back sooner, but he'd only seen a couple of cars on his way, and neither of them had been inclined to stop. Nate would be furious. This would be the third time in as many weeks that he'd missed work or been late.

Andrew and Nate were identical in every way, physically. Both were over six feet tall, with tawny blond hair, dimples, and crystal blue eyes that all the sons had inherited from their dad. But that seemed to be where the similarities ended. Nate was older by three minutes and took the role of firstborn seriously, a little too seriously if you asked Andrew.

He was very much a type-A personality who liked order,

had a plan for everything, and liked to be in charge. In some ways, Andrew was his polar opposite. He liked to take things as they came, rarely had a plan, and felt stifled under too many rules and schedules. He'd always lived life a little recklessly, and his mother had paid the ultimate price. His twin had never let him forget that.

Resigned to the earful he would get, he bypassed the main house and headed straight to the horse barn where he knew his twin would be. Nate had a routine, and he rarely strayed from it. Better to get the tongue-lashing out of the way. Then he could work off his hangover and anger on some remote part of the ranch away from everyone.

As predicted, Nate was in the horse barn. He'd already made quick work of mucking out the stalls and adding the fresh straw. Andrew checked the feed buckets as he passed by the first few stalls. They were already filled. He let out a small groan. Nate must really be annoyed if he'd already finished all that by now.

He found him around the corner by Thunder's stall in the shoeing area. Nate had the black stallion's foreleg trapped between his and was busy shaving the outer layer of the hoof with a razor-sharp hoof knife. Andrew stayed where he was so as not to interrupt his brother's concentration. Too many times he'd been careless or distracted with a hoof-knife and taken off a good patch of skin when he missed the hoof.

Nate would already be upset with him for being late, so he didn't want to make matters worse by causing him to injure himself. He leaned against the stall while he waited for his brother to finish.

Nate finished the horse's hoof with a wire brush and gently

set the leg down before he spoke. "'Bout time you showed your face around here." He spoke softly, but his tone was anything but kind. He wasn't one given to flashes of temper, that was more Andrew's MO, but there was no mistaking the cloud of anger in his blue eyes. They were like shards of ice, piercing and unrelenting.

An excuse was on the tip of his tongue, but for the first time in a long time, Andrew couldn't bring himself to lie or place blame elsewhere.

For nothing is hidden that will not be made manifest, nor is anything secret that will not be known and come to light.

He dragged a hand roughly through his hair. Now was not the time to have an attack of conscience, especially twice in less than twenty-four hours.

"Cat got your tongue?" his brother barked as he quickly and efficiently put the new shoe on.

"No," Andrew answered sullenly. As comebacks go, it was weak, but he really didn't have anything else to say. He was tired, hungry, and just wanted an aspirin and bed. If he didn't say much, maybe his brother would just let him get to it. But that was too much to hope for. Nate was angrier than he'd first let on.

"That's it? That's all you got? No petty excuse for why you missed work? Again?" His brother continued to lay into him. "I don't need to ask what you were doing since I can smell you from here. And if the broken blood vessels around your eyes are anything to go by, looks like you weren't just drinking but using, too." He stood up and shook his head. "I thought by now you would have…" His words trailed off as he led the horse back into his stall.

But Andrew's ire had grown. His face flushed, he stepped in front of his brother, blocking his way. "Would have what?"

"Nothing. Now move so I can put Thunder away." He tried to push past him, but Andrew sidestepped in front of him again.

"No, I want to know what you were going to say," he demanded as the two brothers stood nose to nose. Identical crystal-clear blue eyes bore into each other as seconds ticked by. The only sound was the soft whinny as Thunder registered the tension between them.

"That's what I thought. It's easy to bluster at someone until they call you out on it. You always were more bluster than anything," Andrew snipped as he shoulder-checked his brother as he walked by him. Andrew didn't bother to turn around when he heard the familiar metal click of the bolt sliding home on Thunder's stall. But what did make him turn was when his brother called his name.

"Andrew."

It wasn't so much that Nate had called his name that made him turn, but it was the way in which he did. The tone was low and solemn. Andrew looked at his brother, really looked at him.

He didn't appear angry anymore. He simply looked worn out and much older than their thirty-one years. Nate stared at the farrier tool as he turned it over and over in his hands. In a low voice, he finished his earlier sentence. "I thought you would have learned your lesson when Mom died. That it would somehow tame your recklessness. But instead of being a wake-up call, you seem to be determined to self-destruct. It's been more than ten years now. It's time to grow up. You didn't care about anyone but yourself back then, and now you don't even care that much. You want to ruin your life by drinking yourself into oblivion or doing dope, fine. I can't stop you. But I'm not going to watch you do it." And with that, Nate walked out of the barn and didn't look back.

Andrew stood there for a long time, unable to move, his thoughts skittering in and out, as his emotions were all over the place. He ran the gamut from shock to anger, to hurt, to anguish. Finally, shame washed over him like an icy tide of self-recrimination. Rather than think about why he felt this way, or if there was any truth in what his twin had said, he saddled his horse Micah and rode him hard and fast across the fields to the north. There were some fence repairs that needed to be done and that would keep him busy and away from people for the rest of the day.

CHAPTER 4

Sydney, Australia – The Hills District
Bzzzzzzz. Bzzzzzzz. Bzzzzzzz.

Wendy was pulled from a deep sleep by the sound of vibrations. It took a moment for her to get her bearings as the lingering effects of lethargy still clung to her. Eventually, she realised the sound that woke her was the sound of Bruce's phone vibrating on the nightstand. Glancing at the clock beside her, she saw that it wasn't even two-thirty in the morning.

She felt the mattress shift as Bruce slid out of bed and answered the phone. He went into the other room, talking low, presumably not to disturb her. He mustn't have known she was awake. She debated whether or not to go to him, but didn't want to disturb him. Plus, he'd let her know who it was. But as she lay there by herself, she began to worry.

Who on earth would be calling at this time of night? After the fateful call about her daughter Paige, and her unexpected passing, Wendy tended to worry a bit more than she used to. The time of the call made her anxious, and she clenched her hands in consternation. She began to fret about the possibilities, feeling it wasn't good news.

Her heart started to thud in her chest, and as she got up to go to Bruce, a wave of dizziness crashed over her. So much so that she had to lie back down on the bed and let it pass. She tried to breathe deeply as her head swam and her stomach rolled. After a minute or two, her head began to clear and she felt well enough to sit again. She chalked it up to her not being fully awake yet and letting herself get worked up over the phone call.

Just as she was about to stand, Bruce padded back into the bedroom. She felt an immediate sense of relief and comfort at the sight of her husband. He'd been such a source of strength for her through Paige's death, her other daughter Natalie's custody battle over baby Elysha, and even her son Simon's pronouncement that he was gay. She didn't know what she would have done to get through the tough times without him. But now it might be her turn to be his rock.

"I'm sorry, my darling, I didn't mean to wake you," he said quietly.

Wendy smiled at his preferred term of endearment for her. "You didn't wake me—I heard the phone. Is everything all right?" She couldn't keep the worry from her voice.

He climbed into bed and pulled her close. His face looked troubled. "I'm not sure. That was Nate. It's Andrew. He's been drinking heavily and has started using drugs again. Seems he's gotten himself into a bit of trouble."

Wendy reached for Bruce's hand. She squeezed it, offering

what little comfort she could. "What kind of trouble? Is he okay?" They'd both experienced significant troubles over the years with their kids and her heart wrenched at the thought of them having to deal with another situation.

"He's really lost and is making poor decisions, and Nate's worried about him. He thought it might be best if I come out earlier than we planned to see if I can't be a bit of a guiding presence for him." Bruce pursed his lips. "Despite being twins, Andrew and Nate haven't always seen eye to eye on things, especially after their mother passed."

Wendy didn't know all the details of the accident, but she knew that Andrew had been the one driving. The authorities had said, although he'd been going under the speed limit, he'd taken a dangerous curve too fast and rolled the truck several times. Both had been wearing their seatbelts, but while Andrew had just sustained some superficial cuts and bruises, his mother had died from the impact of the airbag. Her death had torn the family apart, and it had taken a long time for them to heal. From what Bruce had said, the rift had never really been completely healed between Andrew and his twin.

Her heart went out to Bruce and his family. "Of course, you should go out there as soon as possible. We can easily change your flight."

"Are you sure? I don't want to leave you by yourself." The look of love and care he gave her warmed Wendy's heart. She truly was blessed that this man cared so deeply for her, but he needed to be with his sons right now.

"Of course, I'm sure. And I won't be by myself. I'll have baby Elysha to keep me company, and Simon's just out at the bunkhouse if I need anything. I'll be fine," she reassured him.

"I'll join you as soon as Adam and Natalie get back from Hong Kong."

He kissed her cheek gently. "I'm so blessed to have found you. I thank the Lord every day that he brought you into my life."

"As do I." She smiled sweetly at him. "Why don't we pray for Nate and Andrew?"

"Good idea, my darling." He reached for her hand and they bowed their heads while Bruce prayed.

"Dear Heavenly Father, we come to You with heavy hearts. We know You love our children even more than we do, and so Your heart must also be heavy at this time. Lord, we ask You to intercede in Andrew's life. Let him see that the choices he's making are taking him further away from You and the abundant life that's available to him if only he would choose You. He's still carrying a truck load of guilt. Help him grasp the forgiveness and freedom that's available to him in Jesus. Let his heart be open to You and to Your grace, mercy and love.

"And Lord, give wisdom to Nate to know how to handle him. We pray for safe travels as I go to Texas to be with my sons and their families. As Your servant, I humbly come to You for guidance, strength, provision, and understanding as I face tough choices and hard situations in regards to Andrew. Give me wisdom and clarity to know how to help him and to guide him back ti You. We pray all of this in Your holy name. Amen."

"Amen," Wendy repeated softly. "That was beautiful, my love." Her voice choked as she squeezed Bruce's hand, and tears leaked from the corners of her eyes as memories of the anguish she'd experienced over her children surfaced.

"Thank you, darling." Pulling her close, he rubbed her back and gently kissed the side of her head. "Shall we try to get some sleep? We can make the travel arrangements when we get up."

She nodded, and as they nestled into the covers, she snuggled against him. Although her mind still lingered on Andrew's troubles, her heart was light with the peace of knowing they had the strength of the Lord with them, and she soon fell asleep in that comfort.

Later that morning, Wendy made the arrangements for Bruce to fly out the next day. Bruce sent Nate an email with the flight details, and then packed what he thought he'd need for an extended stay. As a sweet surprise, Wendy upgraded his seat to first class. She figured it was the least she could do to help him on his journey. If he was flying halfway across the world because his son was in trouble, he might as well do it in comfort.

Bruce stood in their bedroom with his suitcase almost overflowing and looked around the room. "I feel like I'm forgetting something."

Wendy grinned at her husband. "Don't worry. If you forget anything, just let me know, and I'll bring it with me."

He caught her grin and gave her one in kind. "You're such a treasure, Wendy. What would I do without you?" He crossed the room and enveloped her in his big, strong arms. "I'm going to miss you, darlin'."

She rested her head against his broad chest. "It's only for a couple of weeks," she said as she gazed up at him. He tilted his head down to hers, and she was again caught by the beauty of his eyes. The blue was crystal clear, and right now they shone with so much love, her heart burst with joy. This man was hers, and he loved her with every fibre of his being. She was so blessed.

Rising on her tip toes, she kissed him softly on the lips. "It'll go by quickly. I promise."

He smiled and squeezed her once more before letting her go. "I know. But it'll be the first time since we began our courtship that we'll be apart for this long." He lifted his hand and brushed a stray tendril of hair off her cheek. "Let's make a vow never to spend more than a few days apart after this."

She smiled. "Agreed. Now, finish packing while I call Natalie and confirm the details about Elysha."

"Yes ma'am," he replied, tipping his imaginary hat to her.

Wendy walked out of the room shaking her head and laughing to herself. Her Texan sure was a character. She walked down the stairs and began feeling a bit light-headed. Her foot stumbled on the last step and she started to fall. Thankfully, she was able to right herself by grabbing the banister before taking a tumble.

She was probably just hungry. After the late-night phone call, she and Bruce had slept in later than usual, and she only had a cup of coffee and some fruit for lunch. Shrugging off the dizzy spell, she headed to make a snack while talking with Natalie.

Wendy had been looking forward to this time for months now. Adam, Natalie's husband, was studying for his Master's degree in education and had been invited to be a keynote speaker at this year's annual 21CLHK conference. The 21st Century Learning Conference in Hong Kong was a big deal to attend, and an even bigger deal to be invited to speak at.

The conference drew leading educators from around the Asia-Pacific region and K-12 educators and administrators from more than thirty-three different countries around the world. Run by world-class educators and influencers, its mission was to "Build Communities of Learners." In addition to the annual conference, the 21CL organisation also provided consultancy services for schools and education groups with a special emphasis on the use of technology for the administration of education, learning, and teaching. It was quite an honour that Adam had been invited to speak.

Not only would he get a Certificate of Attendance to go towards his CPD hours, but he'd also get to network with some of the top educators in his field. It was a fantastic opportunity to make connections that could only help him further his career once he graduated. And since he was invited to be a keynote speaker, he was allowed to bring a plus-one at no extra expense.

He and Natalie hadn't been on a proper vacation together since their honeymoon many years ago. Adam had been diligently working on his Master's, and they'd struggled through several rounds of in vitro fertilization unsuccessfully that had taken up much of their time. Then with Paige's unexpected death, they'd become adoptive parents to Elysha. But now that the baby was six months old and given a complete bill of health from the paediatrician, the trip was the perfect time for the couple to get away for some much-needed alone time. Not to mention it was the perfect excuse for Wendy to babysit Elysha.

While she made a sandwich, she made a quick call to Natalie to finalise the details of their trip. Natalie had already emailed her several times with various instructions on how to care for Elysha. Wendy had to laugh at how detailed they were, right down to which tab on the nappy to fasten first. She'd teased Natalie about it. "You do know that I've raised three children, don't you? And quite successfully, I might add."

At least Natalie had a good sense of humour about it. She'd laughed right along with her mum. "Yes, Mum. I do realise that you might have done this a time or two. I'm just a bit of a nervous-nelly leaving Elysha for the first time. But there aren't any safer hands I could leave her in than yours and Bruce's." At that time, they hadn't known that Bruce would have to fly out to Texas early, but when Wendy mentioned it to Natalie, she assured her daughter that everything was still fine.

"Don't fret, and no, you don't have to change your plans," Wendy said as she talked her daughter down from staying home. "I'm not really alone. Simon's staying in the bunkhouse, so he's on hand. And Robyn's offered to stay with me for a few days too. She's over the moon at the idea of seeing baby Elysha. So, there's nothing to worry about."

"I'm pleased Robyn's coming. I'm sure you'll enjoy your time together—she's been such a good friend to you."

"Okay. I'll stop fretting. Thanks again for doing this, Mum. Adam and I are really looking forward to some time alone. We love Elysha, but a short break will do us a lot of good. We'll see you in two days' time when we bring her over."

"I can't wait!" Wendy replied.

CHAPTER 5

The following morning, Bruce woke before the first rays of dawn spilled through the curtains. His heart had been heavy with concern for Andrew, keeping him awake most of the night. He felt particularly helpless being thousands of miles away, and even though he'd prayed for peace, he still slept poorly. He just wanted to be in Texas already and be with his sons.

Bruce glanced over at his wife, but Wendy still slept peacefully. Thankful not to have disturbed her, he slowly rolled out of bed and tiptoed into the master bathroom. Shutting the door softly, he took a long hot shower and reflected on the day ahead.

Emerging from the shower, he was surprised that Wendy's night light was on but her side of the bed was empty. The smell of bacon wafting up the stairs brought a smile to his face. She was singing one of her favourite hymns, *Great is Thy Faithfulness*, as she banged pots and pans around in the kitchen. He'd told her it wasn't necessary for her to get up for him. His flight was very early and he'd wanted her to rest, but she'd insisted that she take him to the airport. He smiled again. He could always count on her to be there for him.

Quickly dressing, he double-checked his carry-on and made his way downstairs. "Something smells delicious." He came up behind her and nuzzled her neck.

She chuckled and shooed him away as she finished scrambling the eggs. "The aroma of bacon works every time."

"I was talking about my beautiful wife, but the bacon smells good, too."

"Well, aren't you the charmer." She laughed again.

He enjoyed the fresh pink blush of pleasure that spread across her cheeks. He'd never tire of seeing her smile. They'd both experienced enough pain for two lifetimes, so it felt good to be a part of her joy.

He sat at the breakfast bar and watched her finish up. Switching off the stove, she wiped her hands on her apron, and proceeded to prepare two plates. After setting his in front of him, he diligently waited for her to sit down with him. He never ate before her. If she was willing to put the time and energy into creating such delicious meals, the least he could do was be patient and share them with her.

After Wendy poured them both a glass of orange juice, they bowed their heads and Bruce gave thanks.

Raising her head after he finished, she asked him if he was all packed and ready to go.

"Yup, I double-checked my bags before I came down to eat."

"And you have your tickets and your passport?"

His Wendy was a planner and he smiled at her insistence

on making sure everything was in order. "Yes, ma'am. The tickets are tucked in my passport and both are right here in my coat pocket," he said as he patted the breast pocket of his vest.

"What about…"

He put a calming hand on hers and squeezed gently. "I have everything I need. Why don't we just enjoy our breakfast since it'll be our last one together for a few weeks. I don't want to spend it worrying."

"Of course. I'm sorry." She returned his squeeze.

They finished their breakfast in companionable silence as the first rays of the sun broke through the low-lying mist, casting a kaleidoscope of soft colours across the hills.

He helped with the dishes and she only checked his bags and travel items once before they loaded everything in the car and headed for Sydney International Airport. The drive was uneventful and they made great time, missing all the traffic crossing the Harbour Bridge because of the early hour.

Since they had time to spare, Wendy suggested he park the car so she could sit with him before his flight. He found a spot and then, after walking to the terminal together, he checked his bags and collected his boarding pass. They decided to have a cup of coffee before he went through security.

Sitting together at a little bar top at one of the coffee kiosks, they people watched while passengers scurried by in silence. Bruce appreciated that they could find peace in each other's company, but it wasn't long before his mind turned to Andrew. He hadn't heard from Nate since he'd called to say he'd be coming to Texas sooner than originally planned. Nate hadn't said anything more about Andrew, only that he was glad his dad would be there soon.

Reaching out her hand, Wendy squeezed his wrist. "What is it, darling? Thinking about Andrew again?"

She knew him too well. He nodded. "Yes, I was just wondering if things were any better. Nate didn't say much else when I called, though I could hear the relief in his voice." He drew a long breath. "I just want to be there now."

"I know, darling. Waiting is the hardest part." It was comforting that Wendy knew exactly what he was going through. How many times had she been anxious about her own children, and especially Paige? She met his gaze. "Why don't we pray before you go?"

"Good idea, my darling."

They clasped hands, and this time, Wendy led them in prayer, her voice soft and gentle. *"Dear Heavenly Father, we humbly come before You, seeking not just peace but Your guidance. We know You're in control of all things, and as the Psalm says, 'Under His wings you will find refuge,' so Lord, we seek that refuge with You now. Cover Bruce with Your wings, and let him find peace there as he flies home to be with his family."*

She squeezed Bruce's hand again before continuing.

"God, grant Bruce the serenity to accept the things he cannot change, the courage to change the things he can, and the wisdom to know the difference. I pray all these things in Jesus' precious name. Amen."

"Amen." Bruce's voice was thick with emotion and his eyes glistened with the sheen of unshed tears. He smiled at her. "Thank you, darling. I needed that."

She slid off the stool and came around to embrace him. This time it was he who laid his head on her shoulder. They stayed that way for another moment before he sighed heavily and raised his head. "I hate to say it," he kissed her tenderly on her forehead, "but it's time for me to go."

Wendy swallowed hard. "I know. I'm going to miss you so much. Make sure you call as soon as you land."

"I will." He gazed lovingly into her eyes as his hands rested lightly on her shoulders. "I love you, Wendy."

"I love you, too."

He lowered his mouth and brushed his lips across hers before pulling her tight again for one last embrace.

Stepping away, he picked up his bag and stole another kiss before leaving her and heading through security. It was only about a forty-five-minute wait before he was called to board the plane and then only another twenty minutes before they were taxiing down the runway. He was pleasantly surprised to discover that Wendy had somehow managed to switch his seat from coach to first class. It was an unnecessary gesture, but as he faced more than fifteen hours of flying, he appreciated having the extra room and the reclining seats.

He'd brought the iPod he'd received for his birthday and Wendy had loaded some audiobooks on it for the flight, including his devotional. Once they reached cruising altitude and the captain turned off the 'Fasten Seatbelt' sign, he leaned his chair back and passed the time listening to the books. At one point he must have fallen asleep because when he awoke, the flight attendant was coming by asking everyone to put their seats up and their tray tables in the upright position to prepare for their descent.

BRUCE LIFTED the shade and blinked a few times as the bright

Texas sun shone through the window. It was mid-afternoon Texas time, and according to the pilot, it was seventy-two degrees. Warm for October, even in Texas. Bruce said a quick prayer of thanks for the safe journey and anxiously waited as the plane landed smoothly and taxied to the terminal. Being in first class, he was one of the first to disembark.

He easily spotted Nate at the gate. His son was tall like him, but he also favored the large Silverado style cowboy hats that he did too. Bruce would recognize that hat anywhere having given it to his son for his twenty-fifth birthday. Nate caught sight of him and waved him over. The two men hugged in the middle of the airport, the depth of emotion shared in the strength of their hug.

"You look good, Pop. Real good. Australia has done you well," Nate said, stepping back and casting his gaze over his dad.

"Thanks, son, but I think Wendy's had a hand in that, too."

Nate nodded. Although reticent at first of Bruce's trip to Ireland and his decision to travel around Europe with a woman he'd just met, when Nate met Wendy and saw the positive changes in his father, he'd quickly come around.

The two men chatted about mundane things as they walked to the luggage carousel to get Bruce's suitcase. Nate insisted on carrying it for his dad.

"Son, it has wheels. I can handle it just fine."

"I know you're capable, Dad. Just let me do this for you. It makes me feel good."

Bruce had to chuckle at being outmaneuvered by his son. How was he supposed to argue with good manners? "Very well. Lead the way."

Bruce didn't fancy sitting in the car for an hour after getting off the long-haul flight, but they passed the time talking about the ranch and the improvements the boys, mainly Nate, and his wife, Alyssa, had made. In the beginning, Bruce and Faith, his first wife, had bought the two-thousand-acre ranch to raise cattle, which they did successfully for about twenty years. However, when the boys became older and the price of grain began to rise exponentially, Bruce had to figure out something different.

Nate always had a head for business and was the first to broach the subject about expanding the cattle ranch to a resort ranch. At first Bruce was dead set against it. Having been a cowboy all his life, he detested the corporations that had tried to come in and buy out the ranches to either make fancy game hunting ranges or develop the land for theme parks. But with a little research and a lot of patience, Nate had been able to get Bruce to come around.

They agreed to keep Cedar Springs as a working cattle ranch but provide lodging and activities for small groups. Initially, they rented the bunkhouse out a few times a year and took small groups and families on guided horseback rides, as well as allowing fishing in the twenty-acre lake that was stocked with bass, crappie, catfish, and a whole lot more. Eventually, they added duck and white-tail deer hunting. As the business slowly built a reputation for being a true Texas ranch experience and not the polished corporate money-making theme-parks that had popped up in the bigger cities, they started getting requests for larger parties.

They added on another bunkhouse that had twelve rooms and a shared community kitchen and game room space. The bunkhouse was rented out year-round and was already booked up for the next eighteen months. They also built mini one-room cabins for renting during the summer as well. There was even a waiting list for cancellations.

They now had a twelve-thousand square foot barn that was used for weddings, corporate events, family reunions, and special occasions. In addition to the fishing, horseback riding, and hunting they originally offered, they now had canoeing, kayaking, and paddle-boarding on the big lake, as well as trail hikes and bird watching around the lake. Guests could also participate in skeet shooting and archery if they weren't into hunting. For families with small children, there was a petting zoo and a smaller stocked pond.

Those who wanted a true cowboy experience could sign up to go on a single day or three-day cattle drive. The guests rode out with the ranch hands and helped drive the cattle from one pasture to another. The single day drive guests rode out at dawn, had a cowboy's lunch, and were back by early evening. The three-day drive allowed for a true cowboy experience, including sleeping under the stars, meals by campfire, and, depending on the time of year, helping with weaning and branding of the calves.

Bruce was in awe of everything Nate and Alyssa had accomplished. Never in his wildest dreams would he ever have imaged that Cedar Springs Ranch would grow to be what it was today, nor as successful. He and Faith had set out to have a piece of land of their own on which to raise their family and to have a business they could one day pass on. God had blessed him with that and much more.

Most of the ride had been spent talking about the ranch,

but as they got closer to Granbury and to Cedar Springs Ranch, Bruce couldn't delay the inevitable any longer. They needed to discuss Andrew.

He finally addressed the elephant in the room and the reason for his coming home to Texas sooner than planned. "So, tell me about what's been going on with Andrew."

He watched his eldest son stiffen at the mere mention of his twin brother's name. His knuckles turned white on the steering wheel as he gripped it too tightly and he clenched and unclenched his jaw before answering. "A bit of the same ole, same ole. Just more often. He's been drinking heavily, and he's started using again."

Although Nate had already told him that, Bruce's heart sank again at the mention of the drugs and alcohol. Andrew had struggled with alcohol and drugs shortly after the accident. Although he never admitted guilt, it was obvious by his behavior that he shouldered a lot of the blame, and Bruce couldn't deny that he too had blamed him at first. Andrew had been the one driving, and Bruce's initial reaction had been one of anger. But over time, God had healed his heart and helped him to realize that Andrew needed his love and support. Not his blame.

But for many months and even a couple years after the accident, Andrew had been beyond reach, finding his solace at the bottom of a bottle. He'd gotten in with the wrong crowd and started staying out all night, getting drunk and being kicked out of bars. There were weeks when he wouldn't come home, and it was on one of those weeks that Bruce discovered Andrew was using drugs. Cocaine, to be exact.

He hadn't come home for more than a week and Bruce

went searching for him. He found him strung out in a dive motel off route I-20. He dragged him out of the hotel and straight into rehab. It had taken six long months and several failed attempts before Andrew sobered up. When he came home, he'd been resentful and within a matter of days, he disappeared again.

Bruce had been grateful when, just recently, Andrew had approached Nate about returning to the ranch. He'd hesitantly agreed, and Andrew moved into the bunkhouse soon after with the ranch hands, although he avoided interacting with the family as much as possible.

Andrew had yet to meet Wendy since he'd refused to attend their wedding in Fiji. Bruce prayed that when Wendy arrived in a few weeks' time and they met, Andrew wouldn't regress even further. But it was a risk they needed to take—Wendy couldn't stay away because of him.

"How long has it been going on?"

Nate took a moment before answering, giving his dad a sidelong glance. "A few months."

"A few months! Why didn't you call me sooner?" Bruce couldn't keep the hurt and concern from his voice.

They pulled up to a red light and Nate met his gaze. It was like looking in a mirror, the same crystal-clear blue eyes staring back at him, only in a younger face. "Because I knew you'd react like this and come rushing home. I didn't want to bother you with everything you and Wendy had going on. Paige's unexpected death, the custody battle. Simon. You had plenty on your plate without worrying about Andrew."

The light turned green and Nate turned his attention back to the road. After a moment, he added, "I thought I could help him see reason, but he doesn't want to hear it from me." His voice grew quiet, almost despondent. "In fact, it seems to only make it worse when I try to talk to him."

"Son, I appreciate you giving us space, but you didn't have to handle this alone."

"But aren't you always telling us that we're never alone?" Nate lifted a brow and gave his dad a sidelong glance. "'God is with you, wherever you may go and no matter what life brings?'" Bruce was pleased to see a hint of a twinkle in Nate's eyes as he quoted the scripture.

Some of the tension in the car eased with Nate's Bible quip. "While that's true, son, it doesn't mean you don't lean on family when things get tough. That's what families are for. And as for Andrew not listening to you," Bruce paused in thought, "well, he's always been that way, even when you two were no bigger than tadpoles. He always wanted to be the oldest and didn't like being told what to do, especially from you." Bruce scratched his head. "I'm hoping I can get through to him."

"I hope you can," Nate said solemnly, the smile gone from his face. "Before he goes too far and does something he can't come back from."

Me too son. Me too. But Bruce didn't say those words out loud. He didn't want anyone but God to know just how scared for his son he really was.

CHAPTER 6

Bruce had only been gone just over a day, but the house felt extraordinarily empty without him. To help fill her time before baby Elysha came, Wendy ensured the house was clean from top to bottom. On her way home from the airport, she'd stopped at the local stand and bought some fresh vegetables. Since Elysha was now seven months old, she was eating baby food, and Natalie and Adam were big advocates of preparing all-natural baby food as opposed to store bought. Wendy was happy to abide by their wishes. She'd made her children's baby food when they were young, and now, the prospect of making it for Elysha brought back sweet memories.

Elysha was also crawling, which meant she had to baby proof the house, or at least the areas where the baby would be. She'd bought a few baby gates to cordon off certain areas of the house and also purchased plug covers and some cabinet locks for the lower cupboards that contained cleaning supplies and breakables. She was taking every precaution necessary for her granddaughter.

Wendy had just finished scrubbing the kitchen floor and had stood to toss the sponge in the sink when a wave of dizziness hit her. She gripped the edge of the farmhouse sink until it passed. This was the second time in as many days that she'd experienced a dizzy spell, but she'd also been cleaning like a mad woman in preparation for Elysha's arrival, so it was probably the fumes from the cleaning supplies.

Typically, she opened the windows when she cleaned, but it had been raining and the wind had been quite strong. She hadn't wanted to open the house during the storm, so she'd just turned on the ceiling fans to help circulate the air. But that must not have been enough.

She was also flushed and hot from cleaning. She probably just needed a breather. A tall glass of ice-cold lemonade would do the trick. Untying her cleaning apron, Wendy poured herself a glass of the fresh lemonade she'd made that morning. As an afterthought, she grabbed a box of crisps from the cupboard and went onto the screened-in back porch to cool off.

It had stopped raining, but the air was still cool as the sun had yet to peek through the clouds. She put her feet up on the wicker ottoman and munched on a couple of crisps as she sipped the cold beverage. Having some food in her belly calmed her queasiness and the lemonade cooled her throat while the light breeze cooled her body. She felt better in minutes. Kicking off her shoes, she shut her eyes and rested the cool glass against her cheek.

She wasn't sure how long she stayed like that, but Wendy

was pulled from her thoughts when she heard the front door slam and a voice call out.

"Mum? Are you here?" Simon's voice rang from the foyer.

"Out the back on the porch," she called out. Moments later, footsteps sounded on the floorboards.

"What are you doing out here?" Simon poked his head around the corner.

"Enjoying the cool breeze. I was cleaning the house in preparation for Elysha's arrival this afternoon and decided I needed a break. Would you care to join me? There's more lemonade in the fridge."

Simon's shoulders fell. Although he lived at the farm, things were still a little strained between them. A lot had transpired since he'd come out as gay at the time of Paige's death. It had been a complete shock to Wendy, and she'd struggled to come to terms with his proclamation. Even more unsettling was when he announced that he was going to marry his partner.

Just as she struggled with his sexuality, so did he. She'd prayed for him every day and trusted that God would work in his life and lead him to the light. And He did. Feeling torn and lost in his heart, Simon had called off the wedding and recommitted his life to Christ, but it was still a long road for both of them. He was still discovering his true identity as a child of God while he dealt with his sexuality. As much as she wanted to push him to stay, she didn't pressure him. He talked with her more often than he used to, so she was grateful for that.

"That's okay if you can't," she said. "I was going to lie down and try to take a nap before Natalie arrives with Elysha, anyway. We can catch up another time." It wasn't a lie, since she'd been planning on taking a short nap after her cleaning, but Simon's impromptu visit had made her forget her intentions for a moment.

Simon seemed relieved for the out. "Thanks, Mum. I will next time. I just stopped by to drop off your mail. I picked it up on my way in. I left it on the kitchen counter." He leaned over to give her a quick kiss on the cheek. "Get some rest. You look a bit flushed. I'm sure a nap will do you good."

"Thank you, sweetheart." As she watched him leave, her heart ached. He still seemed so lost. She wanted to reach out to him, but God was working in his life, and she was sure He had something wonderful planned for him. She just had to be patient and keep praying.

She rinsed out her lemonade glass and put it in the sink. It was one o'clock. There were four hours before Natalie would arrive with the baby. Plenty of time for her to take a nap and grab a shower and be nice and refreshed.

Wendy crawled into bed and curled up on Bruce's side. She could still smell his cologne on his pillows and it made her smile as she drifted off to sleep.

THE RINGING of her phone woke her with a start. She sat with a jolt, disoriented. Glancing at the alarm clock, she was shocked to realise that it was past four. She'd slept for more than three hours! Even then, she still felt groggy. It took her a minute to realise her phone was still ringing.

Snatching it off the nightstand she saw that it was Natalie. "Hello…" She tried not to sound as flustered as she felt.

"Mum? Hi." It was Natalie who sounded flustered.

"Is everything okay?" Wendy couldn't help the alarm that crept into her voice.

Natalie laughed. "Yes, sorry. Didn't mean to scare you. I'm running a bit late. Elysha got into the flour and I have to give her another bath before we bring her over."

Wendy sighed in relief.

"I just wanted to give you a heads up that we'll be a bit later than we said. More like five-thirty or six. I hope that's okay."

"Sure, sweetheart. That's fine." That actually worked out perfectly. It gave her plenty of time to take a shower and wake up properly before they arrived.

"Okay, great. We'll see you in a bit."

Wendy hung up the phone and tossed it on the pillow beside her. She ran a hand through her dishevelled hair and took a steadying breath, not knowing why she was so tired today. True, she'd spent the better part of it cleaning, but cleaning had never worn her out this much before. Instead of feeling refreshed, the nap made her groggier. Hopefully, a shower would be just the thing to help wake her. If not, she'd brew a pot of ginger tea to help invigorate her.

Forty minutes later, she padded barefoot into her bedroom feeling much more alert than she had when she first woke up. She opted for comfy yoga pants and a loose-knit long sleeved shirt. Once she deftly braided her hair to keep it off her face, she made her way downstairs. After turning the kettle on for tea, she busied herself with preparing some baby food for Elysha by boiling some carrots and roasting some sweet potatoes to puree.

The kettle let out a whistle signalling it was ready and she poured the steaming water into the pot. She allowed it to steep while she waited for the vegetables to finish cooking. Once soft, she pureed them until smooth, and then, using a funnel, poured the puree into jars. Sealing them, she placed them into the fridge to cool. She'd just finished her cup of tea and was rinsing the dishes when she heard the front door open, followed by some squeals.

"Hellooooo," Natalie called out. It was followed by an adorable "A-yoooooo."

"In here!" Wendy called as she wiped her hands on a towel and turned to greet her daughter and granddaughter.

Natalie bustled into the kitchen, her arms full of baby, nappies, carrier and more.

Wendy rushed over to help. "Here, let me get some of that for you."

"Actually, just take Elysha. She's the only thing in my arms that squirms." As if on cue, the baby started bouncing in her mum's arms and squealing to be put down.

"Come here, sweetheart. Come see Grandma."

Elysha reached out her chubby little arms excitedly, and Wendy eagerly took her from Natalie. She wrapped the bubbly child in her arms and snuggled her face in her neck making the little girl giggle with delight. She smelled like baby lotion and lavender, and Wendy's heart overflowed with love. Elysha was a living breathing memory of Paige and it made her all the more special.

Turning to Natalie, she asked, "Do you have a minute to visit or do you need to get back? I see Adam didn't come with you."

"No, he wanted to, but he had some last-minute adjustments to make to his speech." Natalie gave a knowing smile.

"He's just a wee-bit nervous about being a key-note speaker and wants to make sure everything is just right. I told him I'd hurry back to help him with it."

"Well, that's understandable. Give him my love and let him know that we'll be praying for him. Baby Elysha and I will have a grand old time entertaining ourselves. Has she eaten?"

"No, after the mess with the flour and having to give her a second bath, I didn't have time." Natalie pointed towards one of the bags. "I only have a couple of jars of food for her." She looked at Wendy apologetically, "Sorry, I meant to make more, but I just didn't have time. It's okay if you want to buy some from the store. Just make sure it's organic."

"That's okay, sweetheart," Wendy assured her. "I bought fresh vegetables from the market this morning and have already made a batch of sweet potatoes and carrots. So, we should be fine."

"Mum, you didn't have to go to all that trouble."

"It was no trouble. Besides, I used to do it for you kids when you were little."

"You're truly a Godsend. Thank you so much for doing this for us."

"You're very welcome. I'm more than happy to." Wendy walked over to Natalie and gave her a one-armed squeeze. "Now, why don't I show you where to put Elysha's things so you can head back to Adam. I'm sure he's anxiously waiting your return."

"Thanks, Mum. And yes, he is."

CHAPTER 7

Wendy and Elysha quickly settled into a good routine. Elysha was such an easygoing baby, so much like Paige had been when she was a child. Right now, she was chortling away in her high chair as she finished her breakfast of cereal. She'd insisted on trying to feed herself and had succeeded in getting as much in her hair as she did her mouth. But Wendy didn't care. Bath time was just as much fun as feeding time. Elysha especially loved the rubber duckies that floated in the water. She squealed with delight as she splashed with them.

After those things were accomplished, Elysha's eyes grew sleepy.

"Are you ready for a nap, sweetie?" Wendy rocked the baby in her arms.

Elysha stared up at her with big blue eyes. She was calm in Wendy's arms and would be asleep in a matter of minutes. Wendy was about to lay her down when a quiet knock sounded on the door. "I wonder who that could be," she said as she glanced out the side window.

It was Colin, Elysha's biological father who now worked on the farm and helped Bruce out with many of the chores and the animals. So much had changed in him since their first meeting and he'd almost become as much a member of the family as Elysha.

Wendy cradled her in one arm as she reached to open the door. "Colin, what a lovely surprise. Come on in. What brings you up here? Have you come to see Elysha?"

Colin stepped inside the foyer, looking a little sheepish. "Um, well..."

"Bruce told you to check on me, didn't he?"

The blush that crept up the back of his neck was all the evidence she needed. "It's okay. I know he just wanted to make sure I'm okay. You can report back that baby Elysha and I are having the time of our lives."

"Thanks for being so understanding. I told him you'd see right through me. But, he made me promise anyway."

"I know. He can't help himself. Would you like some lemonade or iced tea?" she offered.

"Thank you, but I really can't stay. I've got to see to some fencing and the new load of feed is scheduled to be delivered in just a bit. I want to make sure Jim drops it in the right place this time."

"Well, I was getting ready to put Elysha down. Would you like to do the honours before you go?"

The look in his eyes spoke volumes. Colin had fought for custody of Elysha in the very beginning. Paige had not been forthcoming about her pregnancy after they broke up and he'd only heard through rumours that the baby was his. It wasn't until he went to the hospital and had a paternity test that he found out the truth. He sued for custody and Adam and Natalie's adoption had been put on hold. Ultimately, the courts decided that there was no valid reason why Elysha shouldn't be raised by her biological father. Even though the court stipulated that Colin allow Paige's family to be a part of the baby's life, the family had been devastated.

At the time, he'd been with a girl named Annie, but she split soon after he got custody of Elysha. She'd given him an ultimatum to choose between her or his daughter, but to him it wasn't even a choice. The first week as a new dad had been rough, too rough. He thought he was prepared; he had done all this research online. But nothing could prepare him for the true test of fatherhood, and certainly not single fatherhood. Within a matter of days, he'd called Paige's sister Natalie and offered to allow the adoption to go through. He voluntarily gave up his parental rights so that she could be raised by Paige's sister and her husband.

He'd told Wendy and Bruce soon after they invited him to live and work at the farm that he hadn't been sure what to expect, but he'd never in his wildest dreams expected to be 'adopted' too. Feeling compassion for him, they'd invited him into their lives, and now, Natalie and Adam allowed him to see Elysha as often as he wanted and even allowed him to take her out on visits by himself. He often took her to a park and fed ducks at the pond.

He'd also told them that he'd never been one for faith, but the more time he spent with the family, not only hearing them talk about their belief in God but witnessing the way they lived it, the more he'd begun thinking about his own faith. He wasn't ready to make a commitment, but he certainly felt something shifting inside him.

"I'd love to put her to bed. Thank you," he replied.

Wendy passed Elysha to him and watched him cradle her ever so gently in his arms. The baby's eyes were already closed, and her breathing had slowed. She would be fast asleep in no time at all.

~

Since spring had been slow to arrive and the water had yet to warm up, Ellis and his friends didn't surf every morning. Instead, they met at the local rec centre and played pick-up games of basketball, volleyball, or pickle ball—whatever was going on when they arrived. It helped keep them active and brought them together. Afterwards, they enjoyed fellowship over a cup of coffee or tea. Some even chose the wheatgrass juices the juice bar offered, but Simon couldn't bring himself to drink something that green.

He'd known Ellis for quite a few months now and their friendship had grown. Though Ellis was older, he wasn't like a father figure for Simon. More like an older brother. He counselled him, but he never pushed. He was a great listener and Simon found himself opening up to him more and more each day. He talked about his struggles with his sexuality and turning away from God after his father's death. Ellis never judged.

Simon admired him as a person. It was Ellis who had inspired him to study to be a counsellor for others who struggled with their faith and with life issues in general. He'd started his internship at The Emmaus Chapel and things were going well, and it gave him a sense of pride at having something to work towards. After losing his job a while back, his confidence had been shaken and he'd lost direction and hadn't been certain what he was supposed to do with his life.

Bruce, his mum's new husband, had offered him work at their farm in the Hills District. He was able to board in the bunkhouse since he lost his apartment after breaking off his engagement to Andy. It wasn't exactly moving back in with his parents because he had his own place, so he accepted. Being a farm hand was hard work. It was physically demanding, and he often worked from sunup until sundown, but it didn't fulfill him. Not like counselling did.

"Penny for your thoughts?"

"Huh?" Simon was pulled out of his reverie and found Ellis grinning at him. The other guys had already left, and it was just the two of them at the table.

"You've been lost in thought for quite some time."

Simon ducked his head. "I'm sorry. I didn't mean to be rude."

"No need for apology. Sometimes it's good to be lost inside our heads for a bit. Is something troubling you?"

Even though Ellis was digging with his question, Simon didn't feel pressured to answer, but he did anyway. He shrugged as he fiddled with the empty glass in front of him. "I just feel like I should be doing something more, that I should have a bigger purpose." His brows pushed together in frustration. "I just don't know what that something is. I have all these ideas, but nothing seems…quite right."

Ellis nodded slowly. "Believe me, I understand. *'Many are the plans in a person's heart, but it is the Lord's purpose that prevails.'* Everything happens in God's time, Simon. Don't force it, but have an open heart to whatever He leads you to."

Simon scoffed good-naturedly. "That's easier said than done."

"Of course. If things come too easy, they probably aren't worth doing." He pointed in the distance at a group of boys playing basketball. "See those boys over there?"

Simon glanced in that direction and back to Ellis. "Yeah, what about them?"

"Right now, they're safe. They're staying out of trouble. But where do they go when the rec closes? Most of them are runaways, orphans, homeless, you name it."

Simon glanced back at the kids, this time looking more closely. Several of them were in need of a haircut, and all of them were in clothes that were showing signs of wear. Most of them were on the thin side and looked like they could use a hearty meal…or two. It pulled at his heart to think about not having a home to go to, or a home that was so broken that you didn't want to go back to it.

He'd grown up in a wonderful, loving home with two loving parents. He'd never known what it was like to go without food, or without love. He couldn't imagine that struggle. "So where do they go?" he finally asked.

"Some couch surf with friends. Some sleep on the streets. There aren't enough shelters for them, and many won't take minors without parental consent. So, they're left to wander the streets at night."

"Why are you telling me this?"

"Because I'm sharing my struggle with you. I've been trying to work with the city and the rec centre to allow them to stay in the gym at night. I've even offered to supervise, but they've said no. The liability is just too great, apparently." He held up three fingers. "Three years, I've been fighting this battle. But I won't give up, because I know it will happen in *His* time." He emphasised the word by pointing to the sky. "Someday, I'll have a place to keep them safe and to counsel them. Until then, I keep fighting for them."

They finished their coffee and agreed to meet the following week. As Simon drove back to the farm, his mind kept wandering back to those kids. What must it be like to feel like you have no place to go? Simon had felt like that when he'd been hiding his relationship with Andy from his mum, but in truth, he was hiding in darkness. He had a safe place to go; he just chose not to seek it out because he knew deep down that what he was doing was wrong. But these kids weren't doing anything wrong, they were just trying to grow up the best way they knew how.

He reached the turnoff for the farm, and instead of pulling into the drive, he stopped alongside the fence line and climbed out of the car. Leaning against the fence, he stared across the paddocks to the hills in the distance. Things were so ordered out here. The paddocks looked like manicured lawns, the horses were well-fed and cared for. They lacked for nothing. He couldn't help but compare them to the kids he'd seen that morning who were neglected, unloved and hungry.

His heart grew heavy, and for the first time in a very long time, he prayed, not just for himself, but for others. *"Lord, I think You might have placed those kids on my heart for a reason. I don't know if You can use me to help them, but Lord, I'm open and willing. I know I've let You down in the past, and I battle my sinful nature and thoughts every day, but I do seek You and I thank You for the cleansing blood of Jesus which wipes away all my sin.*

"Show me the way, Lord, I pray. Let me be a light in the darkness for those kids. I don't know what I can do, but I'm Yours and I'm available." Matthew five, verses fourteen to sixteen came to him. *You are the light of the world. A city set on a hill cannot be hidden. Nor do people light a lamp and put it under a basket, but on a stand, and it gives light to all in the house. In the same way, let your light shine before others, so that they may see your good works and give glory to your Father who is in heaven.*

How he could be that light, Simon had no idea, but he felt inspired and encouraged when he opened his eyes. He may not have the answers yet, but the Lord did and he was sure that He would use him in some way. He felt it in his bones.

He surveyed the land. They had fifteen acres of level land and rolling hills. They also had a bunkhouse and several horses. It had been a new beginning for his mum and Bruce, so maybe it could be a new beginning for those kids as well.

Campfires and horse riding and youth groups flashed through his mind. This farm would be the perfect place for all that. Away from the city and the temptation of drugs and crime. He had a lot of planning to do, and he needed to run it by Ellis, and of course, get his mum and Bruce's buy-in, but for the first time in a long time, Simon felt alive. Like he had something to work towards, and he felt hopeful and encouraged.

CHAPTER 8

Bruce's first night back at the ranch was relatively uneventful. Upon arrival, he'd settled into the guest room on the first floor. Nate had offered the master bedroom that he and Alyssa had taken over when Bruce moved to Australia, but Bruce had refused. He had no desire to displace them from their room, which is how he saw it now. He made the excuse that it was easier for his sixty-three-year-old legs to not have to do the stairs every night. Nate gave him a look that said he didn't believe a word of it, but he didn't argue with his old man. That amused Bruce, because before he met Wendy, Nate had been the one telling him to take it easy following his cancer scare.

The guest room was plenty big enough for him and for Wendy when she came to join him in a couple of weeks. It had its own master bath, so there was privacy. And Bruce hadn't been lying about the stairs. Although he still got around just fine, it was nice to have everything he needed on the same floor.

Thinking of Wendy, he placed a quick call to her. It was a little after four p.m. here, so it would be just after six a.m. there. It would be early, but she'd made him promise to call as soon as he arrived.

"Hello, darling." Her voice sounded drowsy with sleep and made him smile.

"Did I wake you?" He heard the rustle of covers and imagined her sitting up in bed.

"No, not really. Elysha has been moving about for a while and I've just been lying here resting until she wakes fully. How was your flight?"

"It was wonderful. Thank you for the upgrade. Such a nice surprise."

"You're more than welcome, darling. I'm glad you enjoyed it."

They chatted for a bit more and then he heard the baby begin to cry in the background.

"That's my cue," Wendy said.

"I know. Give my love to baby Elysha and enjoy your time together. I love you and I'll look forward to seeing you soon."

"I love you too."

He felt better having talked to Wendy. She made him feel whole again. He missed her greatly already, this being the first time they'd been apart since they'd been married. But it gave him solace to know she was happy spending time with the baby. He also felt comforted knowing that both Simon and Colin were staying on the farm with her and would be there if she needed anything. Plus, she'd be with him in just a few weeks anyway. He was sure the time would go fast.

As he climbed off the bed, the stiffness in his joints reminded him that he'd been sitting for the better part of sixteen hours. A walk around the ranch might do him good. He'd walk down by the lake or see the new addition to the bunkhouse they'd just finished since he had time to kill. Nate had said he'd be busy for a couple of hours but would rejoin his dad for supper. Alyssa and their kids, Larry and Liza, would also be home then too and they'd have a nice big family dinner.

He didn't ask if Andrew would be joining them. Nate had already mentioned that Andrew kept his distance from the main house, preferring to take his dinner with the other ranch hands in the bunkhouse or eat in town at the local diner. Bruce could sense there was more going on between his two sons, but he hadn't pressed Nate on the matter. There'd be time for that later.

Aiden, his youngest son, wouldn't be joining them either. He was a crop-dusting pilot and was currently out near Amarillo on a job, but he'd be home later that week.

Bruce reflected on the life he'd built for his sons as he strolled the half mile down to the lake. He'd been blessed with twenty-five years of marriage to Faith, and the Lord had blessed them with three sons. Though she'd been taken too soon, he was still thankful to the Lord for the time they'd had.

They'd made many happy memories here on the farm. He'd taught his boys to ride a horse, fish, and hunt on this land. Now, his sons were grown and branching out on their own. Nate and Alyssa had been married for seven years and had a five-year-old son and a three-year-old daughter. They were a lively pair and kept their parents on their toes. It made Bruce's heart swell with pride to know that his grandchildren were building their own memories on this ranch.

The gravel path split at the end of the drive. To the east was the lake and to the west was the bunkhouse and the horse barn. Something told him to go west. He could always see the lake another day. He didn't dwell on why he felt compelled to go this way. He just let his feet carry him in that direction. There was no agenda to follow and he soon came upon the horse barn. Soft whinnies came from within.

Sliding the heavy barn doors open, he stepped inside and was filled with pride at what he saw. The stables were clean and smelled of fresh straw. Each horse had feed and fresh water. All the tack and saddles were oiled and put away neatly on the racks on the wall. He'd taught his sons to take pride in their work, and here it clearly showed. He caught a glimpse of a dark gray and white muzzle poking his head out and smiled to himself. Gus was his oldest horse at twenty-two and one of the favorite choices for the trail rides because of his calm nature.

"Well, hello there, Gus. Been a long time, ole' boy," he said as he rubbed the horse's muzzle.

As if in agreement, Gus bobbed his head and whinnied. In a show of playfulness, he nudged Bruce's shoulder.

"I know. I've missed you, too. But I found me a pretty filly and I followed her back to Australia. You understand, don't ya?"

Gus whinnied again and Bruce laughed. Sometimes he swore Gus knew exactly what he was saying. He scratched the horse behind his ears and gave him a treat before heading out. He'd just closed the barn doors when a gust of wind blew from the east carrying the smell of smoke. Not just any smoke, but cigarette smoke.

Anger boiled inside him. He detested smoking, not just because of the negative health effects, but because it was also extremely dangerous to be doing near a barn full of hay. Who would be that careless? He stormed around the side of the barn to confront the fool.

A cocky young man leaned against the backside of the barn about to take a drag. Bruce seethed as he hurried toward the man. "Put that out right now!"

He couldn't see which ranch hand it was because his cowboy hat was pulled low over his eyes, but it wasn't one he recognized. This guy had tattoos on his hands and gave the impression of self-indulgence and arrogance.

Anger turned to shock when the man casually turned in Bruce's direction. Not bothering to heed Bruce's warning, he took a long drag from the cigarette before answering. "Well, hello to you, too, Dad."

Bruce stopped in his tracks, anger quickly changing to shock and confusion. "Andrew?"

Andrew laughed as he finally put the cigarette out and walked towards him. "Don't act so shocked. Or did you not even recognize your own son?"

Bruce couldn't miss the sarcasm in his son's voice. "It wasn't that I didn't recognize you. I'm just surprised that one of my own sons would be fool enough to light up a cigarette this close to a barn full of hay. Don't you have any concern for Gus and the other horses? Not to mention the fact that your father survived a bout of cancer, and yet here you are putting that cancer stick in your mouth on purpose."

As Andrew sauntered closer, Bruce got a good look at his middle son, the younger of the twins. His hair was much longer now and looked rather unkempt. It hung past his collar in greasy strands and he sported an earring in both ears. Those were new since the last time Bruce had seen him. So were the spiderweb tattoos on his hands. His complexion wasn't much better. It was red and ruddy, a clear indication of too much drinking.

"Relax, Dad. It's an e-cigarette. There's no flame. And as for the cancer, you didn't get it from smoking."

"That's beside the point, but why would you even risk it? The medical profession say that e-cigarettes are even worse than the real things."

"I'm sure they say a lot of things." Andrew's tone was dismissive. After a moment, he bit out angrily, "Why are you even here? I thought you and Wendy weren't coming for another couple of weeks."

The way Andrew spit out Wendy's name hurt a little, but Bruce opted not to fight that battle yet. He knew Andrew struggled the most with his new marriage and he wanted him to have a chance to meet and get to know Wendy. If anyone could change his mind, it would be her. Bruce was here for a whole other reason. "I came because I was worried about you."

Andrew's lips flattened momentarily. "Nate tattling on me again? I'm fine."

"That's not what I hear, son."

"And what's that you hear?"

"That you've taken to drinking again… a lot. And that

you've been using as well." Concern marred Bruce's voice as he asked quietly, "Is it true?"

Andrew's chin jutted defiantly. "Leave it to Nate to stick his nose in my business, where it doesn't belong."

"He's just concerned about you and so am I."

"Nate's never been concerned about anyone but himself!" Under the anger, Bruce could hear the pain in his son's voice, and it tore at his heart.

"That's not true," he argued. "If he didn't care, he wouldn't have called me in the middle of the night."

"That wasn't concern, that was embarrassment and annoyance. He'd much rather I'd died instead of Mom."

Bruce's mouth fell open in horror. "Son, that is in no way close to the truth." He reached out to put a consoling arm on Andrew's shoulder, but he jerked away. If he wasn't mistaken, Bruce thought he saw the glimmer of unshed tears in Andrew's eyes.

"Well, it's been an awesome homecoming, but I've got somewhere to be." Andrew stalked past his father.

"Don't be like that. Why don't you have dinner with me and Nate, Alyssa and the kids?"

Andrew paused but didn't bother to turn around. "Thanks, but I'll pass on the Brady Bunch family reunion. I'll see you around, Pops."

Bruce let him walk off. He was unsure of how to reach him but knew he shouldn't press him right now. Things were much worse than he'd suspected, but he'd just gotten here and didn't want to make the mistake of trying to fix everything right away. If he'd learned anything about life, it was that things happened for a reason and they happened in God's time. He just had to be patient.

As he walked back to the main house, wise words from Proverbs came to mind. *Trust in the Lord with all your heart and lean not onto your own understanding. In all your ways acknowledge Him and He shall direct your path.* He may not know exactly how to help his son, but he could certainly trust God to lead him. He prayed quietly as he walked.

"Lord, Andrew's hurting and he needs Your love more than anything right now. He's wrestling with long term demons. Would You wrap your arms around him and hold him tight? Let him know how much You love him. Send Your angels of mercy to him and shower him with Your comfort. And keep him far from those whose words and actions are of no comfort and pull him further from You.

"Let him seek You, Lord, for You alone can free him of his guilt and all that weighs him down. It breaks my heart to see him punishing himself. Show me how to reach him. I pray all of these things in Your precious Son's name. Amen."

CHAPTER 9

Where had that outburst come from? He hadn't meant to spill his guts like that to his father, or to anyone for that matter. But it had just come tumbling out. Anger and pain still rolled through Andrew as he sped down the dusty gravel road of the ranch. He turned the corner to the main road a bit too fast, sending gravel flying everywhere, but he didn't care. He headed east into town. He didn't have a destination in mind but he needed to get away from the ranch. *And Dad.* It felt too crowded with him there.

A drink would be nice, an eight-ball even better. But his father's words rang in his head. The entire conversation had been rough, but he couldn't help but notice the disappointment in his dad's eyes when he asked if he was using drugs again. It would have been easier to take if his father had struck him. But Bruce McCarthy had never laid a hand on his sons his entire life.

Moisture pooled in Andrew's eyes and he angrily wiped it

away. Crying was for the weak, and he wasn't weak. So what if his palms were sweaty and his hands were shaking at the wheel because it had been more than twenty-four hours since he'd had a drink. He didn't need one, he just wanted one. That was different. But even he couldn't delude himself. The truth was there in front of his eyes. His brother had seen it. His father had seen it. Even he himself could see it. He needed help, but he had no idea where to go to get it.

He drove on for a few miles, unsure of where he was going when he saw the sign for Delia's pass by. Without a second thought, he slowed down and did a quick u-turn. Pulling into the parking lot, he shut off the engine and sat there for a moment, unsure of what had made him turn around until he saw Melody, the waitress who'd helped him out the other night.

His stomach rumbled too, reminding him that he hadn't eaten all day. Maybe a hearty plate of food would help settle the nausea he felt. Besides, now was as good a time as any to apologize properly for his behavior and to thank her for her kindness.

The bell tinkled as he walked in. It was mid-afternoon and still a bit early for the dinner rush, but the place had a few customers. Another waitress by the name of Eloise, according to her name tag, greeted him and asked if he was waiting for anyone or if he was alone.

"Just me today," he answered gruffly before checking his tone.

"Well, would you like to sit at the counter?" she asked politely, despite his surly attitude.

He paused before replying. "Actually, I'd like to be seated in

Melody's section." He tried not to blush as Eloise raised a brow at his request. But she didn't say anything other than 'follow me.' He guessed she was pushing at least sixty, but she didn't show it. She maneuvered through the tables and chairs with the speed and agility of a woman half her age. Andrew had to lengthen his stride to keep up.

"Here you go. Melody is in the back with an order, so I'll fetch you something to drink while you're waitin'. What'll you have?"

"A coke would be fine. Thank you." Feeling edgy and fidgety, he thrummed his fingers on the table while he waited. He was grateful when Eloise returned with his drink fairly quickly, because it gave his hands something to do while he waited for Melody. She finally came through the kitchen doors, her arms laden with plates of food. He tried to sneak a glance while avoiding meeting her gaze.

He was in awe of how she could handle all those plates at one time. She didn't drop one as she threaded her way to a table and set each plate down in front of the correct person. She smiled as she chatted with the customers. It was readily apparent that she knew them by the easy manner in which she spoke.

She was a petite thing and probably wouldn't even come up to his shoulder when standing side by side. He was too stoned the other night to have noticed. Her long dark hair was pulled back from her face in a braided ponytail, probably to keep it out of her way while she was serving. Her hazel eyes were alight with laughter and her smile lit up the room. She had a pretty smile. The small gap between her front teeth was cute and only added to her attractiveness.

Melody looked up briefly from the table and made eye contact with him. Her smile never faded, but the expression in her eyes changed a little. It dimmed a bit. Disappointment flooded through him. He desperately wanted to change her mind about him, but he just wasn't sure how to go about it. Apologizing would be a good way to start.

As she said her goodbyes to the table and made her way over to his, his palms began to sweat. His throat suddenly became dry and his tongue felt like sandpaper. He wished for a strong drink more than anything right now, but he quickly pushed the thought away.

"I see Eloise got you a drink, so what can I get you to eat?" She was all business. There was a smile on her face, but it was tight-lipped, and her tone held none of the warmth it just had for the other table.

Andrew swallowed thickly. "Um…"

"Do you need a few more minutes?" She tapped her pen against her pad impatiently.

"Yes…No."

She stopped tapping her pen and regarded him with one cocked brow. Andrew immediately felt foolish.

"Which is it?"

"I know what I want to order."

She waited, looking at him expectantly.

Why was this so hard?

"First, I wanted to say thank you…" When she still didn't say anything, he continued. "For the other night, for helping me when I…" He trailed off not wanting to finish his sentence.

She did it for him. "When you were drunk as a skunk?"

An uncomfortable laugh escaped him. He tried to smile and

use his charm. "Well, I wouldn't say drunk as a skunk. Has anyone ever seen a drunk skunk?" Nothing, complete deadpan from her. "And I wasn't that drunk, I was just mostly tired from a long day of work. I, uh, work as a ranch hand at Cedar Springs Ranch and Resort. You know the place?"

"Yeah, I know the place. And I also know a drunk when I see one. And you were beyond drunk. Using too, if I had to guess."

Shocked, Andrew immediately tried to deny the accusation like he did with his family. "You don't know what you're talking about." But he wouldn't meet her gaze, the shame at being called out too great.

"Oh, I don't?" She put her hands on the table and leaned over to look him in the eye. He couldn't tear his gaze from her hazel eyes that were brimming with fire. "My father was a junkie. Heroin and coke were his poisons of choice. He'd shoot up every day all day. My mother is an alcoholic. Can barely go a day without hitting the bottle. So, I know exactly what I'm talking about." She paused, and her gaze raked over his disheveled appearance. "And judging by your pallor, sweaty palms, ruddy nose, and bloodshot eyes…I'd say you're both. Not to mention your hands haven't stopped shaking since you walked in."

Andrew just stared at her wide-eyed. Any excuse had long died on his tongue.

"But if you want to drink yourself to death or overdose, that's your business."

Dark ugly contempt rolled through him. It crept up the back of his throat like bile and choked him. It felt as if all the layers had been peeled away and he was bare without his shield of bravado and lies. His heart beat erratically and he couldn't catch his breath. His chest rose and fell harder as a new level of shame washed over him. She saw right through him and it absolutely terrified him.

Mumbling an excuse, he scooted out of the booth as quickly as he could. She jumped back from the table in surprise to let him out. He fumbled in his wallet for some bills and threw a couple on the table, not even bothering to look. He just knew he needed to get out of there. So, he fled. Fled from the diner, from her, from his demons.

He didn't even remember getting in his car or picking a direction. He was too lost in thought, or too lost trying not to think, that a lot of time had passed before he became aware of his surroundings. He was on a back-country road that wound its way along a river and it looked vaguely familiar.

Andrew passed an old wooden sign that read *Dinosaur Valley State Park* next right. Memories of family vacations flooded back. This had been his mom's favorite place to take him and his brothers when they were little. They got a kick out of searching for dinosaur tracks in the riverbed of the Paluxy River. When they weren't finding fossils, they spent their time swimming, fishing, and hiking in the state park.

He wasn't sure what had made him come this way, but he turned right at the entrance to the park and followed the signs to the trails. He parked and got out, and then headed to the Overlook trail. It was one he knew well.

It wasn't a long trail, but it steadily inclined for about half a mile. Andrew had worked up a bit of a sweat when he finally came to the clearing where the lookout was. He probably should have brought some water with him, but when he'd left the diner, he hadn't had a destination in mind.

It was a popular spot, but he hadn't passed a soul on the trail and there was no sign of anyone else, which he was appreciative of. He didn't feel like company at the moment. He sat on the same outcropping of rock he and his brothers had fought over so many times before. Up here on his perch he had a perfect view of the Paluxy River Valley down below.

The sounds of the river below soothed him. A quiet rush that helped calm the roaring of his heart and mind. Sitting by himself, there in that space, emotion overcame him. Melody's words came back to him. He didn't know why it was her words that had struck a chord, because he'd heard them all before, but this time he couldn't turn a deaf ear.

He hadn't been trying to kill himself, at least not intentionally. But, if he were honest with himself, that's the path he was headed down. Nothing good would come from a life of drugs and alcohol. He didn't want to die, he just wanted to numb the pain.

Tears pooled in his eyes and solemnly streamed down his cheeks. Not trying to stop them, he just let them fall. Sitting on that rock, sobbing like a child, all the grief and sorrow he'd been storing up for over a decade bubbled to the surface.

He'd never gotten over the accident that had taken his mother's life. He'd never forgiven himself and didn't think that he deserved to be forgiven. His callousness had taken a life, a life of someone he loved more than life itself. No number of apologies could change that.

Come to Me, all who labor and are heavy laden, and I will give you rest. Take My yoke upon you, and learn from Me, for I am gentle and lowly in heart, and you will find rest for your souls. For My yoke is easy, and My burden is light.

The words came to him as if they'd been spoken out loud. Lifting his head, he searched for the source of those words, but he was completely alone. But he didn't feel alone. It was as if a hand was on his shoulder, offering him comfort. Immediately his heart felt lighter.

It had been years since he'd believed in God, and even longer since he'd tried to talk to Him. The last time was when he'd lashed out in anger after his mother's funeral. He hadn't tried since then. He didn't think he had the right to ask God for help.

I loved you at your darkest.

"No!" he cried out. "I don't deserve Your love."

For all have sinned and fallen short of the glory of God. He has delivered us from the domain of darkness and transferred us to the kingdom of His beloved Son, in whom we have redemption, the forgiveness of sins.

Andrew pondered those words. He knew what he'd been taught in Sunday school, but how did he feel about those teachings now? How could he be forgiven for all the things he'd done wrong, especially killing his mom? If only he could. He'd harbored the guilt for too long and was more than ready to be relieved of the burden, but how to make that happen? Asking God to forgive him for everything seemed too simple.

In the same way, the Spirit helps us in our weakness. We do not know what we ought to pray for, but the Spirit himself intercedes for us through wordless groans. Trust in the Lord with all your heart and lean not onto your own understanding. In all your ways acknowledge Him and He shall direct your path.

In that moment, Andrew knew what he had to do. On that rock, in the middle of the park, he kneeled and lowered his head down, and for the first time in a long time, he prayed. His voice wobbled and tears welled in his eyes. *"Heavenly Father, it's been a long time."* He paused. Blew out a breath.

"I lost my way and I messed up badly, but I want to find my way back. I don't deserve Your forgiveness. You know my heart and You know my struggles. I'm not strong enough to stop using on my own, please help me. Give me Your strength. I don't know what the next step is, but I want to take it. Show me the way back. In Jesus' name. Amen."

He remained still before God, eyes closed. Like the water flowing over the rocks below, cleansing them, he felt something wash over him, cleansing him. When he opened his eyes, his heart was lighter and his head clearer than in a long time.

The steps of a good man are ordered by the Lord, and He delights in his way. Though he fall, he shall not be utterly cast down; For the Lord upholds him with His hand.

Andrew didn't know what the next day would bring, but he'd come to a turning point in his life, and it felt good.

CHAPTER 10

The day finally came for Wendy to fly to Texas and to meet up with Bruce. Anticipation filled her as Natalie hugged her at the airport drop off.

"Are you sure you wouldn't like me to come in with you, Mum?"

"No, it's fine, sweetheart, but thank you. No sense getting the baby out. Let her sleep," Wendy replied, returning Natalie's hug.

Elysha was sound asleep in her baby seat in the back of the minivan. She looked so adorable, and Wendy would have loved to have hugged her one more time before she left for Texas, but she'd only just fallen asleep. She'd have to get her snuggles when she and Bruce returned.

"Have a safe flight, Mum, and call me when you land, okay?"

"I will, sweetheart." Wendy waved to her daughter one last time as she headed into the terminal. Although sad to leave her family, especially baby Elysha, having spent the last two weeks with her, she was more than ready to see Bruce. Even though they talked on the phone every day, it wasn't the same as being with him.

She made her way to the ticket counter to check her bags. The smartly dressed attendant greeted her warmly as she took Wendy's paperwork. "Welcome, Mrs. McCarthy. I see you've been upgraded to first class. That also entitles you to complimentary drinks and appetizers in the VIP lounge while you wait for your flight to board."

Wendy frowned. "Sorry. Did you say I've been upgraded? Is it a promotion or something?"

"No, ma'am." The attendant's manicured nails clicked on the keyboard while she typed. "It says here that Mr. McCarthy requested the upgrade a few days ago. Is everything okay?" She seemed puzzled by Wendy's reaction.

Breaking into a grin, Wendy chuckled softly. "Yes, everything's fine. Seems my husband's returning a favour." Thanking the woman, she grabbed her boarding passes and headed through security with a light heart. Fancy Bruce doing that!

Having plenty of time to kill before her boarding time, Wendy decided to take advantage of the VIP lounge. Settling into one of the plush chairs, she ordered a sparkling water and Caprese salad. She didn't mind flying, but didn't want anything heavy on her stomach. While sipping the cool refreshing beverage and enjoying the light meal, she people watched. Such an interesting past-time, she could do it all day.

Half an hour later, the call came over the loudspeaker that her flight was pre-boarding for first class passengers. Gathering her things, she made her way to the first class line and boarded. The plane took off without issue and she settled in for the long-haul flight to Texas. The upgrade was wonderful. Although not a tall woman, just average height, she still enjoyed being able to recline her chair back more than just a few inches.

She settled in with one of her all-time favourite movies, *When Harry Met Sally*. The flight crew came by with dinner, but, feeling a little nauseous, she declined the meal and asked instead for a few bags of pretzels and some ginger ale to settle her stomach. She fell asleep sometime during *You've Got Mail*. She'd purposely picked the late afternoon flight so she could sleep during most of it and be refreshed when she arrived in Dallas mid-afternoon.

Her plan worked quite well, and she found herself being gently awakened by the flight attendant as the plane started to make its descent into the Dallas/Fort Worth International Airport. She must have been more tired than she thought because she still felt a little light-headed when the plane landed and taxied to its terminal. However, her excitement at finally seeing Bruce overshadowed her grogginess.

Amongst the first passengers off the plane, Wendy spotted Bruce right away. How could she miss her handsome Texan with his favourite wide-brim cowboy hat, or the giant bouquet of yellow roses in his hand? Quickening her pace, she stumbled into his arms as her light-headedness returned. Thankfully, he caught her before she tumbled. She didn't care that he crushed the flowers to her back as he enveloped her in his arms and pulled her close. It was simply wonderful to be with him again.

"Careful, darling. I don't need you taking a spill on me

now," Bruce whispered into her ear, sending shivers down her spine.

"I'm okay, just a little groggy from the flight. Haven't got my land-legs back," she joked, though the dizziness had barely ebbed. She leaned into him as much for support as for the connection. How she'd missed him! They held each other for a few seconds more before she pulled back and lifted her gaze to his.

His eyes glistened as they gazed into hers. "It's so good to see you, Wendy. I've missed you so much."

"And I've missed you, too."

"Oh, dear. I'm afraid I may have crushed these flowers." His cheeks blushed a light shade of pink as he brought the flowers around to her. The bouquet was only a little worse for wear, with just a few petals having fallen off.

"They're beautiful," she said as she brought them to her nose and inhaled the soft honey scent. How many men would think of doing something so sweet? She was so blessed.

"Shall we get your luggage?" he asked as he extended his arm.

"Yes." Grateful for his arm, she clung to him as they strolled to the luggage carousel. In no time at all, they'd collected her luggage and were on their way to the car. At one point, she swayed against him, and he again asked if she was okay, concern etched in his voice.

She played it down. It had to be the flight. What else would it be? "It's nothing, darling. I haven't had a full meal since yesterday—I only snacked on the flight. I'll be fine as soon as we get settled at the ranch and I can eat a real meal."

"We'll be home in just over an hour. Nate and Alyssa are

going to grill so there'll be plenty of food. I'll call him now and let him know we're on our way."

"Sounds good. I'll call Natalie and let her know I arrived safely."

They each made their respective calls to their kids as they made their way to the car. Thankfully, Bruce had parked in the thirty-minute parking lot, so it wasn't a far walk. After placing the luggage in the boot, he helped settle her into the front seat.

"Tell me about the ranch and the kids. How is everything?" She didn't specifically ask about Andrew, figuring she'd let Bruce ease into that topic in his own time.

"Well, the ranch is doing well. They've added onto it since I've been gone. There are six more one-room cabins by the lake and those will be ready to rent next Spring. The new bunkhouse is done and already booked for the next year. Nate has done a great job of managing the ranch. He's also added a cattle drive experience and a small petting zoo. Weddings are scheduled every weekend for the next nine months. It never ceases to amaze me what he comes up with."

Although Wendy could hear the pride in his voice as he spoke about the ranch and about Nate, she couldn't help but notice that he'd left Andrew out of the conversation. She tentatively pressed the issue. "And Andrew? How is he?"

Bruce was quiet for a moment as they made their way out of the city. He let out a long sigh before answering. "Worse than I thought."

"Oh, darling." She laid her hand on his arm. "I'm so sorry."

He gave a wan smile. "I knew it was bad. Nate wouldn't have called me otherwise, but I didn't have any idea of just how bad he is. He looks terrible; he's thin to the point of gauntness, and his complexion is sallow and ruddy at the same time." He let out a heavy sigh. "I haven't figured out how to reach him yet. He's still so angry, and I'm pretty certain he's drinking and using drugs again. He doesn't look good, and I'm worried for him."

There was nothing worse for a parent than to have a child in pain, physical or emotional, and know there was little that could be done to relieve that pain. Wendy had gone through something similar with Paige. Distraught and angry when her father died, she'd reacted badly and taken to drinking and staying out all night with all sorts of people. Wendy had been fraught with worry as she'd desperately tried to reach her daughter. In the end, all she could do was pray that the Lord would protect her and guide her home, which He did, in His time, not Wendy's. Such a lesson of patience and trust.

"I know you are, darling. We'll pray for him together, and I'll be here to support you in whatever way you need." Wendy wasn't sure how else she could help Bruce, but at the very least she could pray for him and his sons.

"Thank you, darling. I don't know what I'd do without you." Bruce's voice was gruff with emotion.

"Nor me, you." Wendy swallowed hard and changed the subject to a more positive one. "I'm also looking forward to seeing the rest of your family and grandchildren. How is Aiden doing?"

Bruce's tone changed as he enthusiastically told her that Aiden was doing well. "He's got a job crop-dusting for McConnell Agricultural Inc. They serve the majority of the farmers in Northern Texas and parts of Oklahoma."

"That sounds amazing. You never did tell me how he got into crop-dusting."

Bruce grinned. "Oh…Aiden has loved planes since he was a little tyke. Always been fascinated by them. I used to take him to the airshow every year and he'd watch the planes fly all day. When he was fifteen, he asked if he could get his pilot's license. Said he wanted to fly planes for a living. His mother was dead set against it." Bruce glanced over at Wendy. "Faith was terrified of flying. Any vacation we went on had to be within driving distance. Said she wanted to keep her feet firmly on the ground." He let out a small chuckle and faced the front. "But, she eventually came around. Aiden can be very convincing when he wants to be."

"It sounds like the apple doesn't fall too far from the tree." Wendy gave him a coy grin. "I seem to recall a very earnest someone convincing me to travel around Europe with him after we'd just met. And then asking me to marry him!"

His face broke into a broad grin. "Well, us McCarthy men know a good thing when we see it. I didn't want to wait any longer to spend the rest of my life with you. I never thought I'd find love again and I wasn't about to let you go."

"And I'm very glad you didn't." She grinned back at him, her heart warming at the memory.

After a while, she asked if Aiden was seeing anyone. She'd entertained hope early on that Bruce's youngest son and her Paige might have gotten together after hitting it off in Fiji at their wedding, but that never eventuated due to her passing.

"Funny you should mention that. I just found out he's sweet on the next-door neighbor."

Wendy smiled. "That's wonderful. Who is she?"

"Her name is Kimberly, and her family has lived next to ours for almost as long as we've lived there. They moved in about a year after we did. They have two sons, and then Kimberly is the youngest. She used to follow all the boys around everywhere, used to drive Aiden nuts. Growin' up, he always thought she should be playing with other girls, not tagging along with her brothers to our house. But she'd have none of it. She's a fighter that one…had to be." Bruce's tone grew solemn.

"What do you mean?"

He drew a long breath and stared straight ahead. "Her father passed away in a farming accident when she was twelve. Then both her brothers enlisted in the Army and were stationed in the Middle East. She only got to see them maybe once a year. So, it was just her and her mom."

"That's so sad. I can't imagine what it would be like to grow up without a father." Wendy had been blessed to have both her parents in her life. They'd been married fifty-four years before her father passed away, and then just a year later, her mother followed him to be with the Lord, too.

"That's not the half of it. She studied hard and got herself a scholarship to the University of Texas Law School. She was well into her second year when her mom got sick."

"Oh, no. Please don't tell me she lost her mum, too."

Bruce shook his head. "By the Lord's grace, Karen survived, but it was touch and go for a while. She thought she had the regular flu, but it progressed quickly. Ended up being bacterial meningitis, and it was a strain that was resistant to antibiotics. She started having liver and kidney failure and was put on the transplant list. Kimberly dropped out of school and came home to care for her mom."

Wendy's hand went to her throat involuntarily. "Oh, how difficult that must have been for her. She must be one resilient young lady."

"That she is. She and her mama both have a strong Christian faith that helped guide them through those troubled times. Karen recovered and is doing quite well now. But Kimberly decided to stay here with her and is a paralegal in Dallas. From what I hear from Aiden, she's taking night classes so she can finish her degree."

"She sounds like a strong, independent young woman. I can understand why Aiden would be taken with her."

"Me too. They're good for each other."

"I can't wait to see him again, and to meet Kimberly."

Bruce turned his head and grimaced. "Unfortunately, you won't get to see him for another week since he's out on a job."

"That's a pity, but I'll look forward to catching up with the rest of the family in the meantime."

"You won't have long to wait. That's the gate to the drive just up ahead."

Wendy shifted her gaze and her breath caught. She'd seen pictures of the large, ornate wooden arch spanning a long gravel drive with the words 'Cedar Springs Ranch & Resort' carved on top, but in real life, it looked amazing and so, so impressive.

"Home, sweet home," Bruce announced with pride.

CHAPTER 11

The first night on the ranch, Wendy hadn't just been re-introduced to Bruce's eldest son Nate and his wife Alyssa and their two kids, she'd been accepted into their family with open arms. Looking very much like his father with the same crystal-clear blue eyes, Nate also shared Bruce's laugh. Although more stoic than his father, he was still very much the charmer.

Alyssa was a sweet woman, the epitome of the 'southern charm' that Bruce often referred to. She was a gracious host and Wendy was made to feel comfortable almost immediately. Over the following week, the two women bonded over their love for gardening, horses, and of course, raising children.

Larry and Liza were the apples of Bruce's eye. Larry was five, almost six, and was missing one front tooth. He loved ranchin', as he called it, and fishin' with his pa. Liza, three going on four, was definitely the quieter of the two. She had her mother's sweet disposition and shared the same striking blue eyes as the rest of the McCarthy clan.

Wendy spent most of her days exploring the ranch with Bruce, reading by the lake, and helping Alyssa prepare the meals. She was pleasantly surprised to find that the Texas growing season extended well into the fall, and she enjoyed helping Alyssa in the garden picking the last of the autumn crops of broccoli, cauliflower, and squash. The children 'helped' too, but often got distracted by butterflies and frogs.

The fresh air and relaxation did wonders for Wendy, not to mention being with Bruce again. They spent the evenings sipping sweet tea on the front porch and watching the fireflies dance at dusk, and she hadn't had another dizzy spell since getting off the plane, which proved to her that she'd simply been overdoing it. Maybe she'd taken on a little too much by herself, but now that she was with Bruce, he encouraged her to take it easy and to simply enjoy the break.

She'd even taken to riding in the mornings while Bruce helped the boys with the morning chores, a big step since she wasn't an experienced rider. But something about being at the ranch gave her confidence she'd never expected.

Bruce had chosen a beautiful young gelding, named Sable after the silky dark brown of his coat, for her to ride. He was even-tempered and the perfect mount for her. He seemed to enjoy their leisurely morning walks as much as Wendy did.

She often rode through the pastures to the east side of the property, stopping under a grove of willow trees to watch the sun rise above the horizon and burn off the morning dew. The birds sang happily, while other wildlife began to stir. It was a time of joy, bringing to her mind the verses in Ecclesiastes:

A TIME TO REJOICE

There is a time for everything, and a season for every activity under the heavens. A time to weep and a time to laugh, a time to mourn and a time to dance.

Wendy's time to weep and mourn Paige's death had come and largely gone, although sometimes grief still snuck up on her, taking her unawares, and she would burst into tears at the most inappropriate of times. Her grief would never leave her entirely. She knew that, but having baby Elysha in their lives helped greatly. The baby was such a joy and a delight. So now was Wendy's time to laugh and dance, perhaps not literally, but being out there on Sable, surrounded by such beauty, peace and joy were slowly replacing her weeping and mourning.

TUESDAY MORNING, Bruce and Nate left early to go into town for the cattle auction, so Wendy decided to take her ride earlier than usual. She dressed warmly since the mornings were still chilly and headed to the barn. She wasn't worried about getting Sable ready. Someone was always in the barn at dawn since work started as soon as the rooster crowed, as Bruce often liked to say.

She pulled the large barn door back and let her eyes adjust. Sable must have been thinking about her, too, because he was already up and poking his head out of the stall, whinnying. She smiled when he bobbed his head as she approached.

"Well, good morning to you, too. It's early for you to be so cheerful."

"I was going to say the same thing to you."

Wendy jumped at the sound of the unfamiliar voice. Although she knew there'd be a ranch hand or two in the barn, for a moment, she'd forgotten. She turned to see who it was who'd spoken to her. A tall man with long hair pulled back in a ponytail and wearing a number of earrings peered at her. When he came closer, she caught wind of body odour. Maybe he'd been hauling hay or something and had already worked up a sweat. Whatever had caused the smell, it was quite unpleasant.

"Sorry, I didn't mean to startle you. I wasn't expecting company this early." He stepped into the light and Wendy recognised the eyes—the same as Bruce's, though his were red-rimmed and bloodshot. He resembled Nate, but he was on the thin side, where Nate was broad-shouldered and muscular from years of farm work. This must be Andrew, his twin.

Wendy smiled gently. "I'm sorry, I couldn't sleep. I thought I'd take Sable for an early morning ride, if that's okay."

"No skin off my back. It'll give me a chance to clean out his stall while you're out. I'll saddle him for you."

"Oh, it's no trouble. I can do it myself if you're busy."

"My father would tan my hide if he knew I let you saddle your own horse." His voice was resigned and even bitter.

"You must be Andrew," she said softly.

"And you're Wendy." His eyes narrowed speculatively as he studied her. Neither made a move to shake hands. Finally, Wendy stepped forward and extended her hand. "It's nice to finally meet you. Your father speaks highly of you."

Ignoring her hand, his mouth twisted in a wry grin. "I somehow doubt that."

She wasn't sure what to say to that, but she didn't get a chance to respond because he turned and walked to the tack wall to grab what he needed and started saddling the horse.

Deciding some things were better left unsaid, she went to fetch a riding helmet and left him to finish saddling Sable.

Once done, he helped her onto the saddle and let her out of the barn. "The fog gets heavy this time of year near the eastern fence and down by the lake. It might be best if you stick to the western trail that goes by the apple grove. There's a small incline, but you'll be out of the fog."

She gave him a grateful smile. "Thanks. I'll bear that in mind."

Nodding, he left her and turned to saunter back into the barn.

Wendy could see why Bruce was so concerned. Andrew definitely had some demons he was fighting. His eyes were bloodshot, and there were dark circles under them as if he hadn't slept in a day or two. At least he was courteous, even if he'd been a little gruff. And they'd finally met. She'd gotten the impression he'd been avoiding her since she arrived. Putting him out of her mind for now, she gently nudged the horse forward. Sable responded and headed down the gravel drive.

Reaching a fork, she thought of Andrew's advice. Although she loved the trail by the lake and the sounds of the frogs, she thought it best to heed his words, so she nudged Sable to the west. Passing the apple grove, she enjoyed the sweet, crisp scent of the Gala apples. The trail began to gradually increase as she left the apple grove behind and headed towards the backside of the property.

She'd just begun to consider turning around when Sable stiffened beneath her. "Whoa boy," she said, trying to calm him. Something had spooked him, but she couldn't tell what. *A coyote?* Bruce had told her they abounded in the area, just as dingoes frequented the outback of Australia. She'd never come face to face with a dingo, and she didn't want to come face to face with a coyote, either. Glancing around, she couldn't see any. Breathing easier, she patted Sable on his side, but he flinched and danced in a small circle. Something wasn't right, but what?

Not wanting to stick around and wait for trouble to find her, Wendy pulled on the reins to turn him like Bruce had taught her. It took a bit of coaxing, but he finally turned. They hadn't taken but a few steps before she realised her mistake. She didn't need to wait for trouble to find her, they'd walked right into it. Her breath hitched. A large brown snake lay in the middle of her path, coiled with its head low, shaking its tail while making a rattling noise. Australia had its fair share of snakes, but Wendy didn't recognise this one. Any snake could be dangerous, especially when on horseback. This wasn't good.

Trying to stay calm for Sable's sake, she whispered low to him as she pulled back on the reins, trying to get him to back up slowly. As gentle as the gelding was, he was still young. Fear overrode his conditioning to obey commands, and he whinnied loudly and pawed at the ground in front of the snake—the last thing she needed. The snake coiled tight and then struck out at the horse.

Sable reared. Wendy's heart beat in her throat as she struggled to stay mounted as he pawed and kicked at the air. If only she was more experienced. All of a sudden, she felt herself sliding down the horse. Dread coursed through her veins. The saddle was slipping!

She fervently prayed as she clung on for dear life. With her last ounce of strength, she hauled on Sable's mane and pulled herself and the saddle back on top of the horse, but her hold was tenuous at best. They had to get away from the danger so she could fix the saddle properly.

"Hi-yah!" she kicked the gelding hard in the sides with her heels. It was nothing she was used to, but fear goaded her on. They had to get away from the snake. The horse responded immediately and surged forward. The snake hissed and rattled as they raced by. Too busy hanging on for dear life, Wendy didn't look back to see if it was following them.

Having escaped one danger, she now found herself facing another. The horse was barrelling down the trail at a frantic pace and the saddle was now completely uncinched. Nothing was keeping her and the saddle on the horse except her legs, and they were close to giving out.

She tried desperately to slow Sable, but fear had gripped him. Reaching a bend in the trail, he didn't slow. His hooves skittered in the dirt and rock. He went left and Wendy sailed right. She and the saddle went flying. The saddle landed harmlessly in the grass between two trees, but she wasn't so lucky, slamming into an outcropping of boulders that lined the trail. Thankfully, her riding helmet protected her head as it came down hard against the rocks, but the rest of her body wasn't so lucky. She not only felt, but also heard, the loud crack as her right leg slammed into the boulder.

Searing, white hot pain like nothing she'd ever felt before shot through her. She screamed and clutched her thigh as the pain stole her breath. It felt like someone had snapped her leg in two. Tears streamed down her face as she lay in pain.

She had no idea how long she lay there, because she must have passed out, but eventually, she became aware of her surroundings and could think past the pain. As gently as she could, she pulled herself into a sitting position so that she was leaning upright against the outcropping. Stopping several times, her stomach rolled at the agony caused by moving her leg even a fraction of an inch.

She needed to take stock of her injuries to make sure she wasn't bleeding. Carefully, she unclipped her riding helmet and slid it off before checking there were no head or neck injuries. She had a slight headache from the fall, but the helmet had done its work. There was a large scratch along the right side, but no cracks. Moving as little as possible, she slowly checked the rest of her limbs.

Aside from a long scratch down her right arm that was only superficial, she was more sore than anything else. It was her leg that was the worst, but thankfully, it didn't appear to be a compound fracture. No bones protruded; it appeared the break had been clean. She was thankful for small miracles—it could have been a lot worse.

As for her situation, she wasn't sure it could be much worse than it was. She whistled for Sable a few times to no avail. The horse was long gone. Not that she would have been able to ride him anyway, but he would have been a nice comfort as she waited for help to arrive.

She silently chastised herself for not checking the saddle herself that morning. Not that she felt Andrew had made a mistake on purpose, but she knew better than to not double-check her gear. Bruce had instilled in her the importance of doing this while giving her riding lessons. She also knew better than to go off without her phone. The last time she'd done that was the day Paige died. Since then, she never went out without it, but today she'd forgotten and left it charging on the nightstand. So, here she was, with no water, no food, and no way to call for help. She took some slow breaths and gazed around. All she could see were wide open spaces. How would anyone find her out here?

Just like David sought prayer when he feared for his life with the Philistines, she did the only thing she could think of and bowed her head and prayed. *"Lord, thank You that You're here with me. I pray that You'll help Bruce and the others find me as quickly as possible. Be the light to help them find their way to me. Until then, keep me safe. In Jesus' name, I pray. Amen."*

The pain in her leg was almost unbearable, but there was nothing she could do to ease it, so she hummed worship songs and placed her thoughts on Jesus instead. As tears streamed down her cheeks, she also uttered Psalms and sang hymns to distract herself.

Lying quietly in the shade, she tried to remain calm as the sun rose higher in the sky. The temperature climbed and she began to sweat in her denim jacket. As carefully as she could, she removed the jacket and rolled it into a ball. Using it as a pillow, she rested her head against the cool rock. Surely, Bruce and his family would be there soon. Exhausted, she drifted off into a troubled sleep.

CHAPTER 12

Bruce and Nate had taken longer at the auction than they'd intended, but they'd gotten an exceptional deal on a head of steer they just couldn't pass up. It wasn't every day that a thousand head of prime Texas Longhorns became available. It cost them a pretty penny, but the ranch would make that money back ten-fold over the next three years. It had been well worth the cost.

Bruce was on the phone with the rancher who'd auctioned the steer off, arranging the delivery, when they pulled back onto their ranch drive. Nate pulled up to the barn and left his dad to finish his conversation. He'd just stepped out of the truck when a familiar voice floated from the horse barn. "Leave it to you to arrive after all the chores have been done," his younger brother, Aiden, joked with a smile.

Nate's eyes widened in surprise. "I thought you weren't getting back until tomorrow!" The two brothers strode toward each and clasped in a one-arm hug.

"Lucky for you I got back early, otherwise you'd be shoveling manure until dinner time." Aiden chuckled as he stepped back from Nate and looked around. "Where's Dad?"

Nate nodded to the cab of the truck. "Talking with Joe Richardson. We scored a thousand head of prime longhorn steer from him. Pop's arranging the transport."

Before Aiden had a chance to comment, the sound of horse hooves coming from the far side of the barn interrupted them. As they turned, Sable trotted around the side of the barn, rider-less and saddle-less.

"Looks like you let one escape. Must have left his stall unlocked," Nate joked with his brother.

Aiden's brows came together. "I didn't touch his stall. It was empty when I started and it had already been cleaned out. Sable hasn't been in it all morning."

"Then how did he get out?"

"Beats me." Aiden shrugged.

Nate's lips thinned with anger. "I bet I know. Where's Andrew?"

"In the barn, shoeing Marigold. Why?"

Nate didn't answer. Instead, he stalked toward the barn. Andrew was by the horseshoeing area. Nate yelled for him, but Andrew either didn't hear or he simply ignored him. Irritation simmered hot under Nate's collar. Striding up behind Andrew, he yelled, "Hey!"

Startled, Andrew dropped the file and nearly jumped out of his skin. "What's the big idea? You're gonna scare the horse!"

"You've got bigger things to worry about than Marigold. Besides she doesn't spook at anything. She's half deaf."

"What are you talkin' about?"

Aiden had followed Nate into the barn and stood nearby.

"I'm talking about you being careless this morning and letting Sable out of his stall," Nate said accusingly.

Andrew stood and got in Nate's face. "For your information, I did let him out. But I wasn't being careless. Dad's new woman wanted to go for an early morning ride, so I helped saddle him." He pointed to the empty spot on the wall where the tack and saddle should have been.

Nate felt the blood drain from his face. He grabbed his brother by the shirt collar. "Which trail did she take? Which way did she go?"

Stumbling under his brother's rough hands, Andrew struggled to maintain his balance. "What's gotten into you?" he said angrily, as he shrugged off Nate's hands.

Aiden placed a calming hand on Nate. "Let him go. That's not going to help us right now. He doesn't know."

Nate complied and Andrew smoothed his shirt down with an angry hand. "I don't know what?"

"Sable just came around the side of the barn…by himself. No saddle, no rider. No Wendy."

Now it was Andrew's turn to become white as a sheet. "That's impossible," he said, shaking his head.

Dad joined the group, his brows knitted. "What's Sable doin' tethered outside?"

Nate glanced at Aiden. His face was pale, too. He looked back at his father, but before he could answer, their dad asked what was going on.

Nate looked to Andrew and raised a brow accusingly, but before either man responded, Aiden broke the news. "Wendy took Sable out for an early morning ride. He came back without her."

A range of emotions played across Bruce's face. "Maybe she stopped at the lake to sit on the dock. She likes to do that. Maybe she forgot to tie him up properly. She's probably walking back now. I'll take the truck to pick her up." He turned and headed for the truck.

"Dad, Sable came back without a saddle or tack," Nate said quietly.

Bruce stopped and turned around, his troubled gaze traveling between the three boys. "What are we waiting for? We need to find her." His voice was thick and unsteady.

Nate placed a calming hand on their dad's shoulder. "We will. Aiden and I will saddle up and head out on the horse trail by the lake. You take the truck and follow the main road in case she decided to double back on that."

"I don't think she went to the lake this morning."

Three pairs of eyes turned to Andrew.

Bruce stepped toward him. "What makes you say that, son?"

Andrew shifted uncomfortably under his father's gaze. "I, um...I told her the fog was heavy that time of morning around the lake and I thought it might be safer to head west by the apple grove." He looked down at his feet, scuffed them in the dirt before looking back up at his father. "It's a little higher so there'd be less fog and she'd see the trail better."

"That was good thinking, son." Bruce gave new instructions. "I'll have to take Old Smith Road to get to the apple grove. Nate, you and Aiden, take your horses and follow the trail she would have gone on."

"I can ride out, too," Andrew said, earnestly.

Bruce turned to him. "Someone needs to stay here in case she comes back. Keep your phone on you so you can call us if she does."

The three men headed in different directions. No one saw the look of disappointment and hurt flash across Andrew's face as he was left behind.

While Bruce left to drive around the apple grove, Nate and Aiden hurried along the western trail. There hadn't been rain for a couple of weeks, and the trail was dry. This was both good and bad. It meant the ground was nice and firm and safe for a horse to follow, but it also meant there were no tracks to follow. They only had Andrew's word about his advice from this morning. If they'd chosen wrong, they'd waste more than an hour searching in the wrong direction.

They took turns calling Wendy's name, but there was no response. Within twenty minutes, they'd reached the apple grove. They searched the grove for any sign of her, but found none.

Aiden drew his horse close to Nate's. "Do you think Andrew was wrong? Or that she didn't listen to him. You've met her, and you know her better than I do," he said.

Nate gave a frustrated shrug. "I don't know. She doesn't strike me as the type to not listen or to go off in the fog. I think she would have taken Andrew's advice, but I just don't know. I thought we would have come across her by now. Do you think she went further?"

"No idea, brother. At this point, your guess is as good as mine. What do you want to do? I'll follow your lead."

"I have no idea, either. I think we should pray."

"Good plan."

Nate glanced into the sky and then closed his eyes. *"Father, we need Your help right now. Lead us to Wendy. We have no idea where she is or how to find her, and she might be hurt and in danger. Take our hands and guide us to her. In Your holy name. Amen."*

Nate opened his eyes and looked at Aiden. "I think we should keep going." He didn't see why Wendy would have gone past the apple grove, but he trusted that his instincts were being guided by a higher power, so he nudged his horse in that direction.

About a half-mile past the grove, Nate stopped and Aiden pulled up beside him. "Can you see her?"

Nate sat in silence for a moment as he calmed his heart, sensing they were close. "No, but let's call out again, together, this time."

"Sure."

Nate held up his hand and counted to three, then the brothers called out in unison, "Wendy!" They waited, not daring to breathe as they strained to listen. Nate was about to call out again when he heard a faint sound. Was it 'help' that he'd heard?

The brothers looked at each other, and they called out again at the same time, "Wendy!"

This time, the answering call was louder, and it was definitely the word, 'help.'

Elation and fear rippled through Nate as they urged their horses in the direction of Wendy's voice. He brought his horse to a slow trot as he called out again. "Wendy! It's Nate and Aiden. Call out again so we can track you. Keep calling out."

"Over here! I'm by two big pine trees and a group of rocks. Help!" Her voice was still faint, but they were near. They spurred their horses on, and rounding a bend, they spotted her, propped against a group of large boulders. She was dirty and pale, but she was alive.

Nate quickly dismounted his horse and rushed to her side. "We're so glad to see you!"

"Not as glad as I am to see you." She sounded breathless.

Nate spied the saddle and reins lying near her. "What happened?"

She quickly explained to both men what happened. Curious as to how the saddle had slipped, Nate inspected cinches and wondered if they hadn't been tightened properly. His lips thinned as he met Aiden's gaze before turning his attention back to Wendy. "Let's get you home. Can you ride? Dad's worried sick."

"No, I can't ride. My leg's broken. I can't even move it without excruciating pain."

Aiden stood behind Nate. "I've called Dad. He's going to meet us with the truck, but he can't get all the way back here. We'll have to carry her about a quarter mile."

Neither man had brought any rope to make a splint, so there was no way to secure her leg. Aiden suggested using the reins, but they needed them to tie the horses up with so they didn't wander off. Besides, they didn't have a knife strong enough to cut through the leather.

"It's okay. I've managed the pain for this long, I can manage a few more minutes," she said.

The brothers agreed it would best for them each to support a shoulder and let her use her good leg to help walk along the trail.

Nate felt for Wendy as she put on a brave face while they

helped her up, but she couldn't suppress the grimace of pain when they helped her to her feet. They held her steady while she caught her breath. A fresh sheen of sweat had broken out on her brow. Just the weight of her leg hanging seemed to be excruciating for her, but there was no way to avoid the pain. He and Aiden would have to be as gentle as possible with her as they made their way to their dad's truck.

"Are you ready?" Nate asked softly.

She looked at him with determination in her eyes, gritted her teeth, and nodded for them to continue.

It was slow going. They stopped many times for her to catch her breath, but after what seemed like hours, Nate spotted the truck. Bruce jumped out of the vehicle and sprinted straight for Wendy. As he approached, she succumbed to sobs. Nate and Aiden held her steady as her body shuddered.

⁓

BRUCE WANTED to crush her in his arms, but by the way his boys were holding her upright, he could see she was injured. "Oh, Wendy, my love. What happened?" As gently as he could, he placed a hand to her cheek, dirt-streaked and damp with tears.

She met his gaze but seemed unable to speak.

"It's okay, darling. I've got you." He took over from Nate and helped her to the back of the truck. Learning her leg was broken, he thought it best for her to ride in the bed on the horse blankets. That way, she wouldn't need to bend it, but it would still be a rough ride until they reached the main paved road.

He settled her in the back of the truck as best he could and then climbed in beside her. Aiden sat on her other side to help brace her. Nate drove as carefully as possible, but Bruce had cut across fields to reach her. His heart wrenched with each bump, and each time she screamed out. Her hands were clammy, and her face, ghostly pale. He fervently prayed for God to ease her agony.

It seemed like forever before they reached the paved road. Wendy visibly relaxed as the jostling ceased. At one point she closed her eyes, but Bruce doubted she was asleep. He continued to hold her hand and whisper words of encouragement.

They made it to the hospital in under half an hour and were met outside by an ER triage team who helped her onto a gurney and rushed her into the ER. Nate offered to stay with him, but Bruce insisted he go back with Aiden to get the horses. He also asked them to pack some clothes for him and Wendy in case they had to stay overnight. His sons hugged him quickly before he rushed into the ER to be with her.

∽

NATE AND AIDEN were silent as they drove back to the horses. Aiden offered to take Nate's home so Nate could hurry and pack a bag for their dad and Wendy and return to the hospital.

When Nate pulled into the drive, Andrew was sitting on the front steps. He jumped up and strode to the truck. "How is she?"

His brother's eyes were bloodshot, glassy and red-rimmed, clear indication he'd been using recently. Nate's blood boiled as he pushed the door open and jumped out, jabbing a finger into his brother's chest. "I'll tell you how she is. We found her on the trail, scared and hurt with a broken leg. A snake spooked the horse and her saddle came off. It hadn't been cinched properly."

Andrew's face paled.

"Yes, it was your fault. You were high again, weren't you?" Nate didn't even wait for his brother to object; he just kept after him. "Your carelessness and blatant disregard for your own health and safety put hers at risk. She could have been killed! It's bad enough that you don't care about your own life, but do you have to be so thoughtless and careless to almost take another?"

∽

ANDREW RECOILED as if he'd been slapped. He hadn't been high that morning. He hadn't had a drink or a score in over a week, which was why he had the shakes and wasn't sleeping. Withdrawal had hit him hard, but he was determined to make it this time. That's why he'd been in the barn early that morning. He couldn't sleep, plus, manual labor helped take his mind off his symptoms. He hadn't meant to be careless with Wendy.

The thought of his actions causing her harm was too much to bear. He shoved past his brother and took off around the barn, ignoring his brother's calls. Tears stung his eyes as he jumped in his truck and floored it down the drive, leaving a cloud of dust and sprayed gravel in its wake.

CHAPTER 13

Nate's words kept rifling through Andrew's head like a bad record stuck on repeat. His hands shook as he tried to keep his truck on the road. He didn't know where he was going but he had to get away from the ranch and his brother's accusatory eyes. Part of him wanted to go to the hospital to be with his dad and Wendy, but would he be welcome? After all, it was his fault she was there. Or at least that's what Nate believed. He wasn't sure if his father and Wendy believed that too.

Banging his fist on the steering wheel, he squeezed back the tears that threatened to spill. Even when he tried to do right, he did wrong. He hadn't been high like his brother had accused. But had he been careless? He hadn't meant to be. Would they believe him? Or would they believe Nate?

Would they think he was careless, or would they believe he'd caused Wendy's accident on purpose? He'd not made any attempt to get to know his father's new wife, and even worse, he'd uttered unkind words about his father marrying again. But he could see that Wendy made his dad happy, although he hadn't wanted any part of their relationship to start with. Now he regretted ignoring her.

The familiar neon sign of Delia's came into view, and Andrew found himself pulling into the parking lot yet again. He didn't see Melody or her car, which was just as well. He was too shaken up to face her, but he needed someplace to reconcile his thoughts, and for some reason, this place felt like a second home. It was virtually empty except for one old-timer sitting at the counter drinking coffee and reading the local news. Andrew almost had the place to himself, which was just fine.

A waitress he didn't recognize greeted him, and he asked to sit in the booth in the corner. She popped her gum loudly and shrugged. "Sure, there's no one else here besides Roy." She nodded at the lone customer at the counter. "Sit where you like." She looked disappointed when all he ordered was coffee, but his stomach was too knotted to eat anything. When she returned with the coffee, he handed her a twenty-dollar bill for her trouble. She left him to his own devices after that, only coming by every so often to top off the coffee.

Andrew stared at the window as he thought back to the morning. Try as he might, he couldn't remember if he'd finished saddling the horse correctly or not. Most of the steps were second nature to him, and he wouldn't have had to think twice about getting Wendy's horse ready. But he'd been distracted and hadn't expected any company that early. She'd caught him off guard. That, and he was still struggling with the symptoms of withdrawal. They always got worse before they got better.

Had he missed a step that morning? Lately it seemed all he did was miss a step. It felt like every time he turned around he was headed in the wrong direction. Why did he even bother anymore?

The steps of a good man are ordered by the Lord, and He delights in his way. Though he fall, he shall not be utterly cast down; for the Lord upholds him with His hand.

Andrew had no idea why he thought of that verse just now. He didn't feel worthy of the Lord's help, not before, and certainly not now. He sunk his head in his hands as despair overwhelmed him.

∼

Melody walked into the back of the diner and through the kitchen to clock in for her shift. She gave Tom, the cook, a brief nod before tossing her purse and keys in her locker and grabbing her apron. It had been a stressful day already, and she still had to pull a ten-hour shift. She tied the apron in the back and slammed the locker with a little more force than necessary.

"Something got your petticoats in a bunch this morning, darling?"

Melody spun around to see Delia leaning against the countertop watching her with a sardonic expression. Her boss's brow lifted when Melody didn't answer straight away.

"It's nothing." Nothing she wanted to get into, anyway.

Even though the whole town pretty much knew the situation with her mom, she still felt embarrassed by it.

"Child, I been knowin' you since you were barely out of knickers. Now, if you don't want to tell me, that's fine, but don't lie to me."

Feeling properly chastised, Melody felt her face warm. She blew out a long breath and then apologized. "I'm sorry, Delia. That was rude. It's just Mom again…"

Delia pushed off the counter and put a knowing hand on Melody's shoulder. "Say no more."

In a rare moment of need, Melody let her guard down long enough to lean into Delia's comfort. The older woman didn't say a word and simply waited. She always could read Melody's moods. She didn't need words right now. She just needed a moment's reprieve from the weight of the world she felt she carried on her shoulders. Even if it was temporary, it felt good to know Delia was there for her. Feeling better, she backed away and pretended to smooth down her apron. "So, what do we have going on for tonight?"

Delia rattled off the evening's special, what prep work still needed to be done, and anything Melody needed to know for the night shift. "Oh, yeah, and that guy is here again," she added as Melody turned to go.

"What guy?"

"The drunk guy from the other night."

"Not again." Melody shook her head and rolled her eyes to the ceiling. "Don't worry, I'll get his drunk tail out of here so he doesn't make a scene."

"Leave him be."

"What?" Melody stopped in her tracks, one hand on the

swinging doors. She'd been prepared to march into the dining area full of fire and brimstone and give him a piece of her mind. But Delia's words stopped her.

"He's not drunk this time," she said. "But he don't look good. Been sittin' in the corner booth nursin' cold coffee for more than an hour. Paid Rachel twenty dollars for a spot to sit."

Melody eyed Delia curiously. Her boss was not known to have a bleeding heart, except where she and her daughter were concerned. It was highly unusual for her to allow someone to sit in her diner for hours on end without ordering anything, especially a newcomer like Andrew.

"Leave him be?" Melody asked, unsure of how she was supposed to handle this new turn of events.

Delia shrugged. "He's not bothering anybody, and he looks like he could use a quiet space to work through whatever demons have put that haunted look in his eyes." She didn't say anything more about it, just turned on her heel and walked out the back, leaving Melody standing in the doorway gaping.

Melody busied herself in the kitchen and prep area before she made her way out onto the floor. She wanted to give herself some time to calm down from the fiasco with her mother that morning. She'd come stumbling home drunk at four in the morning and woken not only Melody, but Jasmine, too. It had taken twenty minutes to wrangle her mom into her bed and another twenty after that to get Jasmine settled back into hers.

Melody hadn't been able to sleep after that. So, since she was up, she tidied the house, made a casserole for dinner that night, and folded the rest of the laundry. Once Jasmine was up later that morning, she took her over to Mrs. Bailey to watch her. She didn't need her daughter to see her grandmother hungover. Although Mrs. Bailey was more than willing to watch her under the circumstances, Melody still felt obligated to pay her a little extra since it wasn't her day to keep her eye on Jasmine. There was no way she would trust her mother to watch her daughter in that condition.

She'd have to figure out what to do with her mother later. Right now, she had to focus on her shift. She retied her hair in a ponytail, grabbed her pen and notepad, and headed out to wait on the afternoon crowd that was beginning to shuffle in. For the first hour of her shift, she busied herself with a few tables, but every so often she glanced over at Andrew in the corner. He had yet to look up from his coffee or make any move to leave. From the slouch in his shoulders, he appeared extremely dejected and forlorn.

She couldn't avoid him forever, and something in her heart called out to him. She told Tom she was taking her first break and asked him to watch her tables for her. Grabbing the pot of coffee and a fresh mug, she walked over to Andrew's table. He didn't even look up when she set a fresh steaming cup in front of him; he just kept staring out the window at nothing in particular. Taking pity on him, Melody slid onto the opposite seat.

"Rough day?"

He blinked in surprise as if she'd caught him lost in thought. Probably had.

"Er..." He looked down at his hands and then up again. "Yeah, you could say that."

There were dark circles under his eyes as if he hadn't slept in days and his eyes were red-rimmed, but not from drinking. After living with a drunk for most of her life, Melody could tell the difference. No, his eyes weren't bloodshot from booze. Either he had terrible allergies, or he'd been crying. Based on his expression and demeanor, she figured it was the latter.

He reached for the fresh cup of coffee, and she couldn't help but notice the tremors in his hands. Recognizing the signs of withdrawal easily enough, she took pity on him. "You should probably eat something. It will help settle your stomach."

His expression immediately turned defensive. "I'm not drunk." He glared at her with unrestrained anger.

She held up her hands as if in surrender. "I know you're not."

At her acquiescence, his anger appeared to abate as quickly as it had come. His expression now resembled more confusion and skepticism. "How do you know I'm not?"

"Because I recognize the signs of withdrawal when I see it." She gave him what she hoped was a sympathetic smile. "Lord knows I've seen it often enough. What with a junkie for a father and an alcoholic for a mother."

It was his turn to show her a sympathetic look. "I'm sorry."

"Don't be," she said. "I got through it." She reached a tentative hand across the table and touched his lightly. "And you will too."

Her kindness seemed to be his undoing. When his face crumbled and big tears rolled down his gaunt cheeks, her heart wrenched at the agony that splayed across his face. He didn't remove his hand from hers but let his head fall to his chest, and she watched silently as his shoulders shook with emotion. She gently stroked his hand in comfort and silently prayed for the Lord to give her the right words to say. "It really is going to be okay," she tried to reassure him. "The first step is the hardest, and you've already taken it."

He shook his head as he finally looked up and met her gaze. "It's not that."

Melody frowned. "Then what is it?" If it wasn't withdrawal, why was he so upset?

"Even when I try to do right, everything seems to go wrong." He pulled his hand from hers and cracked his knuckles. "I didn't mean for her to get hurt."

Alarmed, Melody implored, "Who? Who got hurt?"

"Wendy," he whispered through tears. "She fell off her horse and may have broken her leg."

Relief flowed through Melody. Her thoughts had gone to the worst-case scenario and she'd had visions of him driving drunk and killing someone. Thankful it hadn't been that, she continued to question him. "Who is Wendy?"

"My father's wife."

"Your mom fell off her horse?" Melody was having trouble following.

"No, Wendy is my dad's second wife. My mother...she died when I was barely out of high school."

"I'm so sorry. I didn't know."

"That was my fault too." He said it so low, she almost didn't hear him.

"What?" Had he meant he'd caused his mother's death? Surely not.

"My mother died in a car accident; I was the driver." His voice broke as he recounted the story. Melody listened in silence as he retold that fateful day many years ago. Many times, she wanted to reach out to comfort him, but she refrained, sensing he needed to get it all out first.

He told an achingly familiar story of pain, heartache, shame, and guilt that led to drinking and drugs. She may not have experienced firsthand what he'd gone through, or knew what it was like to fight a personal addiction, but she did know what it felt like to love someone who did. She knew the anguish of watching a loved one choose the temporary fix over themselves, or in her case, their children, day in and day out. She knew the destruction that drugs and alcohol caused a person and a family.

When he finished his story, he gazed at her, his eyes watery and imploring. "And now Wendy's hurt, too, and it's all my fault."

"How can it be your fault? Did you push her off the horse?"

Her attempt at being lighthearted fell flat. He looked at her with a blank expression. "No, I didn't push her." Frustration was evident in his voice. "But I was the one who saddled Sable for her."

Melody assumed Sable was the horse. Still not quite understanding how her fall was his fault, she asked, "How did she fall?"

"Her horse got spooked by a snake. She broke her leg pretty badly in the fall."

"That can happen to anyone, even the best of riders," she tried to assure him.

He shook his head. "No, that's not it. She wasn't thrown out of her saddle. Her entire saddle and rigging came undone." He paused. "It hadn't been cinched properly."

Ahhh. Understanding washed over Melody. He blamed himself because he was the one who'd cinched the saddle.

"Okay. So maybe you didn't cinch it correctly." He looked like he was going to argue with her, but she held up her hand. "Let me finish. Maybe the saddle was put on incorrectly, or maybe something else happened. You can blame yourself if you want to, but are you sure Wendy would have stayed in the saddle when the horse spooked, even if it had been cinched correctly?"

He shook his head. "She's inexperienced, from what I understand."

"Right, and I'm sure you know even the best riders can get thrown from their horses. I'm guessing, even if Wendy was an experienced rider, she wasn't familiar with Sable, nor he with her."

Andrew nodded his head, but this time he looked slightly more open to what she was saying.

"My guess is that no matter whether the saddle was correctly secured or not, Wendy might have been bucked off that horse. Maybe I'm wrong, but there's no sense in blaming yourself for something you have no way of knowing was your fault. Did you want her to get hurt?"

"Of course not!" His voice rose with vehemence.

"Then quit blaming yourself." Melody smiled inwardly as Andrew opened his mouth and then closed it again. He had no argument.

"Stay put for a second. I want to show you something. Please?"

"Okay."

She got up from the booth and hurried back to the kitchen.

Opening her locker, she dug in the bottom of her purse for a small, wrinkled pamphlet. She'd planned on giving it to her mother, but she felt Andrew needed it more. Clutching it in her hand, she hurried back to the table.

He watched her curiously as she slid back onto the booth seat and passed the brochure to him.

"What's this?"

"It's a flyer, for an AA meeting."

As he attempted to hand it back to her, she pushed it back into his hands. "Just hear me out, okay? You still don't want it, fine. But just hear me out."

She'd known Mark Waters, the founder of 'Fresh Start', for more than a decade. He'd been a friend of her father's, an old drinking buddy. One day, he'd been out at the bar, having a few beers after work. A few turned into many, and still he decided to drive home. He crossed the double-yellow line and hit a car head on. He was in a coma for three weeks and nearly died. He woke up in the ICU only to find out that the car he'd hit had been his wife's.

His wife had hated when he drove home after being at the bar after work. She'd grown worried when he hadn't made it home by his usual time and went looking for him. He found her first—with the front bumper of his truck.

Melody went on. "He tried to drown his sorrows with pills and the bottom of a whiskey bottle. Was almost successful, too. But eventually, he pulled himself out of the darkness and became an advocate for those in need. He started a group for people struggling with addiction, called 'Fresh Start.'"

Andrew didn't say anything, just exhaled deeply and looked out the window.

Determined to get through to him, Melody continued. "Look, you don't know me from Adam, and I don't know you, but something is telling me you're worth fighting for."

Her last words finally got his attention. He turned his gaze back to hers, the expression in his eyes unreadable.

"Look, I have to get back to work. Take the pamphlet, read it over. You still aren't interested, throw it away. I can get another. But, if you want to go and you don't want to go by yourself, I'll go with you." Melody nodded her head towards the kitchen. "Tom and Delia know how to reach me if you need me."

With that, she slid out of the booth and went back to waiting on her tables. Half an hour later, she glanced over at the corner booth. He was gone, and he'd left without saying a word. Disappointment weighed heavily on her until she went over to wipe down the table and found a hastily scrawled note on a napkin.

I'll think about it.

The brochure was gone.

CHAPTER 14

Dallas, Texas – Baylor University Medical Center
Bruce had been anxiously pacing the hospital waiting room for more than an hour. He'd had no update on Wendy's condition. When they first arrived at the hospital, an x-ray showed that she had, in fact, broken her femur. While it wasn't a compound fracture, it was still a serious injury, and she'd been taken for emergency surgery to fix the break. He had only a brief moment with her before they wheeled her away. He'd kissed her forehead and told her he loved her, and then she was gone behind the double doors.

He'd spent the time alternating between pacing the floor and sitting and praying with his head bowed. Anytime the doors opened, he jumped up in hopes of an update, but so far, none had been for Wendy. He'd considered going to the cafeteria to grab something to eat, but he was too anxious to eat anything. The nurse had offered him coffee, but he'd graciously declined. He didn't need to add caffeine to his already nervous system. He would just have to ride it out and give all his worries to God. Two Bible verses came to mind:

Give all your worries and cares to God, for He cares about you.

Do not be anxious about anything, but in everything by prayer and supplication with thanksgiving let your requests be made known to God. And the peace of God, which surpasses all understanding, will guard your hearts and your minds in Christ Jesus.

'Yes, Lord, I give Wendy into Your hands because there's no better place for her to be.' With his heart a little calmer, Bruce was able to pass the time reading some of the magazines in the waiting room. Before he knew it, another hour had passed, and the double doors opened again. He looked up as he heard someone call his name.

"Mr. McCarthy?" A middle-aged male doctor in blue scrubs looked around the room.

Bruce stood quickly and hurried over to greet the surgeon. "That's me, I'm Bruce. How's my Wendy?"

"Mr. McCarthy, I'm Dr. Walters. I performed the surgery to repair her leg. The surgery went fine. The break was clean, and I was able to reset it with a metal plate and screws to hold it in place while it heals."

Bruce exhaled the breath he'd been holding. "That's wonderful news. Thank you so much. When will I be able to see her?"

"Soon. She's in recovery now and will be there for about another half hour. Then a nurse will take you to see her."

"Will she be able to go home tonight?" Bruce was anxious to see Wendy, but he also wanted to care for her in the comfort of his home.

"Well, we'd like to keep her in the hospital for a couple of days."

Bruce frowned. "A couple of days? I don't understand. You said the surgery went fine."

"We'd like to run a few more tests before we send her home." The doctor didn't quite meet Bruce's gaze when he replied.

"A few more tests for what?" Bruce's gaze narrowed. "What's going on, doc?"

"Nothing yet. It's more precautionary," the doctor hedged.

"If you're worried about something, just give it to me straight." Tending to be a direct person, Bruce would much rather face problems head on.

"Look, Mr. McCarthy…"

"Call me Bruce."

"Okay, Bruce. I don't want there to be any alarm if there doesn't need to be. We did some routine preliminary blood work before Wendy's surgery, and her white blood cell count was abnormally high." He held up his hands before Bruce could interrupt him with a question. "Now, that can happen for a number of reasons. So we are just going to run some additional tests to find the source."

Bruce's heart began to beat double-time. Having survived cancer himself, he knew what an elevated white blood cell count could mean. "When will we know more?"

"Not for at least twenty-four hours."

Bruce felt his lungs deflate.

"I know that seems like a long time, but we need to make sure that she's stable from the surgery and that the anesthesia is fully out of her system so there aren't any false indicators in her blood." The doctor put a reassuring hand on Bruce's shoulder. "Try not to worry about what it could be. It may be nothing."

Bruce wasn't so easily mollified, but he nodded to the doctor anyway. He knew there wasn't anything more the doctor could do right now.

Shortly after he left, a nurse came and took Bruce to see Wendy. She was still groggy from the surgery, but her spirits were good. The nurse said she'd sleep most of the night.

After kissing her and telling her how much he loved her, he took a moment to call Nate to let him know how she was doing, and that he'd be staying with her in the hospital that night. Not wanting him or the others to worry more than they already were, Bruce didn't mention anything about the anomalies in Wendy's blood.

The next twenty-four hours were the longest Bruce had ever experienced. Wendy slept through the night like the nurses said she would, courtesy of the heavy pain medications she was under, but Bruce slept fitfully. Try as he might, he couldn't help but worry about the worst-case scenario. He also worried about how much to tell Wendy when she woke up later that morning. He'd never lie to her, but he didn't want to hinder her recovery if there was nothing to be concerned about. He decided to wait until the doctor knew more before saying anything, so he fell asleep praying that come morning, the news would be better.

The following morning, when Wendy opened her eyes, Bruce raised her hand to his lips and kissed it gently. "Good morning, my darling. How are you feeling?" He swallowed the lump in his throat as he gazed into his beautiful wife's eyes and tried not to think about anything other than how much he loved her.

"Not too bad, considering." She moved slightly in the bed. "Have you been here all night?" Although she was weak, concern for him sounded in her voice.

"I have. I didn't want to leave you."

"That's so kind, but you could have gone home. It's only a broken leg."

Bruce tried to keep his expression neutral, but Wendy must have noticed something in his face because she asked if anything else was wrong.

"Oh, darling. I wasn't going to say anything until we knew more, but the doctor is concerned about your white blood cell count."

Wendy's grip on his hand tightened, her face paling. "White blood cell count?"

He nodded. "I'm sure it will be fine, darling, but he wants to do some tests to be certain."

Their gazes held as unspoken words passed between them.

A nurse came in a little later to draw blood. She put a rush on the order and the results came back within the hour. Wendy's blood still showed a high white blood cell count, and the doctor was concerned about some antigen markers. He ordered a CT scan for later that day.

Bruce spent the next few hours reassuring Wendy that everything would be fine and that he'd have her out of there in no time, but even he could tell that his false bravado wasn't working. Although she smiled with him, worry sat behind her eyes. He wished more than anything he could wipe that worry from her heart.

The CT scan only took fifteen minutes, but they had to wait an hour for the results. When Dr. Walters entered the room, Bruce knew it was bad from the grim expression on his face. Wendy's hand tightened in his as the doctor gave them the news.

"I'm so sorry. I wish I had better news, but Wendy, you have brain cancer. Glioblastoma multiforme, to be exact."

A heavy, invisible weight crushed Bruce's shoulders. He'd already lost his first love, Faith. He never thought he'd find love again, and then he'd met Wendy. And now he was faced with the devastating news that his second love might be dying. It was too much to bear. "How bad is it?" he asked quietly, fighting the nausea in his stomach.

"There's no known cure for glioblastoma, Bruce. Chemotherapy and radiation might slow its growth, but won't stop it. At best, Wendy most likely has between twelve and eighteen months."

Twelve to eighteen months? How was this happening? Bruce's heart slammed into his chest and sweat formed on his palms as the doctor explained their options to 'extend' her life. That's how he put it. Not that they could heal her, but that they could give her a few more months. He left them with some pamphlets and brochures and the promise to talk to them tomorrow after they'd had time to discuss options with each other and notify their family.

AFTER HE LEFT, Wendy sobbed as Bruce held her in his arms.

He dug deep in his faith and harnessed his inner resolve. He had to be strong for her. "Shhh, there now, darling. Don't fret.

We'll get through this." He stroked a hand through her hair as he tried to comfort her the best he could.

"You heard the doctor. There's no cure." Her words came out muffled through her sobs.

His heart wrenched. "There's no *current* cure that they know of. But you also heard him say that medicine is making huge advancements in cancer research every day. Who knows what they'll find in a month or two. Besides, we have something else to help us fight this disease."

Wendy sniffled against his shoulder. "And what's that?"

"Faith." He tilted her head up. "We have faith, and that's stronger than any medicine. You know that our God is all-powerful and all-knowing. He knew this moment was written before we were even born. We can overcome anything if we have faith."

"Oh, Bruce. I don't know if my faith is as strong as yours," Wendy said tearfully.

He stroked her face and brushed the tears from her cheek. "Well, then my faith will have to be strong enough for the both of us. Let me carry this burden for you as the Lord carries ours."

"I love you so much, Bruce McCarthy. I don't know what I'd do without you."

"You'll never have to know." And Bruce believed that in his heart. He only hoped his faith was strong enough for him to believe that he wouldn't have to find out what life would be like without her. "Come now. You need to rest. But first, let me pray for you, and for us."

Wendy nodded. Bruce settled her against his shoulder, clasped her hands in his and prayed.

"Dear Heavenly Father, You know us so well. You created us in Your image. You know the number of hairs on each of our heads, and You even know the thoughts conceived in our hearts before we ever vocalize them. You've told us to come to You and ask for every need of life. You are The Way, The Truth, and The Life, the God who heals, and You have the final word on our destiny, and the number of years we'll live and serve You on earth.

"We're coming to You today as Your children, longing to hear from You and asking for Your divine healing. There's so much we don't understand about life. But we do know that with one touch, one word, You can make us whole.

"We don't always know what Your will is, Lord, especially in times like now, when we desperately seek Your comfort. We offer You no promises, no bargains, no deals to exchange for Wendy's health. We simply bow our hearts before You to tell You the desire of our hearts: that we want to spend as many years as we can loving You here on Earth, loving others, and wanting to become more like You.

"We absolutely believe You have the power to heal. You demonstrated that on earth, and you still heal in miraculous ways today. Even when our faith is weak, You say it is enough, and our love for You is strong. And we know You already hold our hearts and lives in Your hands. If we can bring You more glory through healing, then that's what we ask for. That is what we desire.

"But if Your answer is 'no', or 'not now', we know that Your grace is sufficient for us. Ultimately, we want Your will to be our will. We look forward to spending an eternity with You. But Lord, if You still have more planned for Wendy to do here on this earth, we not only need and want Your physical healing, Lord, but a thorough, deep-down cleansing and strengthening and renewal of all that we are.

"All that we are is Yours. Use this trial to strengthen us from a 'what-if' faith to a 'no-matter-what' faith. And no matter what, we choose to honor You and give You glory. In Jesus' name. Amen."

CHAPTER 15

Wendy was released from the hospital the following day. The homecoming was a rather somber one as the family had been told of her prognosis before they arrived. Andrew was conspicuously absent, having made himself scarce upon their arrival. But Nate and Aiden and Alyssa had all been there to welcome them with open arms. There were lots of tears and hugs, and promises of prayers. It was especially hard for Bruce to watch when Wendy called her children. Her voice broke early in the conversation, and Bruce had to take the phone from her.

He had trouble keeping his voice steady as he told Natalie and Simon that their mother not only broke her leg in a tragic accident, but that she also had terminal cancer. Both her children immediately demanded she fly home to be with them. Once they calmed down, Bruce had been able to reason with them. It simply wasn't feasible for her to fly with a broken femur. The cast went all the way from her hip to her toes, and she was still experiencing bouts of dizziness.

Besides, the doctors had advised that for her best chance at prolonging her life, she would need to start the chemotherapy and radiation right away. Even though Australia had amazing cancer centers, it didn't make sense for her to fly home for treatment when she could also receive the same quality of care in Texas. The University of Texas MD Anderson Cancer Center was one of the best in the country.

Understandably, her family was devastated and wanted to be with her. Bruce offered to fly all of them, Natalie, Simon, Adam, and Elysha, to Texas for Christmas. They readily accepted his offer, and he promised to make the travel arrangements right away.

After Bruce settled Wendy in for the evening, he went out in search of Andrew. He'd not bothered to show his face all day, and Bruce reckoned he felt guilty. Nate had pulled Bruce aside shortly after their arrival and told him everything that had happened in his absence, including the ugly words that had been exchanged between him and Andrew. Bruce wanted to make sure Andrew was okay.

He found him skipping rocks in the moonlight down by the lake. Bruce walked toward him, making sure his footsteps were loud and clear. Andrew didn't say anything as Bruce settled next to him, just threw another stone. Both men watched the stone skip seven times across the moonlit water, the ripples spreading out across the lake.

"You always did have the best arm out of all of us."

"Still do."

Bruce smiled and felt a glimmer of hope. When he first

spotted Andrew down by the lake, he hadn't been sure if he'd be receptive to company. Bruce took the sarcastic remark as a sign that he was at least willing to listen.

"Beautiful night. Mind if I stay here for a bit?"

"It's your land. You can do what you want."

Bruce didn't miss the pain behind the sullen tone. Andrew had always used anger to hide his hurt.

Andrew started to throw another rock, and Bruce said, "It wasn't your fault, son."

Andrew's arm faltered. Bruce watched as he let the rock slide out of his hand, then he clenched his fists at his side. "How can it not be?" He turned and glared at his father. "I was the one who put the saddle on. She was hurt because of me."

Bruce wanted to put his arms around him. There was so much pain in his son's eyes, but as soon as he touched him, Andrew took a step back.

"You saved her." Bruce said.

Andrew's eyes widened. "Saved her? How? She's dying!" His voice echoed out across the still waters.

"We don't know that, son."

Andrew scoffed. "She has a BRAIN TUMOR, Dad. Nate told me. Yeah, she didn't die from the broken leg, but now she's dying of cancer."

"She's not dead yet!" It was Bruce's turn to raise his voice, which he so rarely did. Taking a calming breath, he reminded himself why he'd searched Andrew out. "I came down here to thank you."

"Thank me...for what?" Andrew asked.

"Since you're determined to believe her fall was your fault, then it was your fault that saved her. If she hadn't gone to the hospital with the broken leg and we hadn't found out about the tumor when we did, it would have continued to develop at a rapid pace, and I'd maybe have weeks with her instead of months. And who knows? God can do all things. He can heal her of this terminal cancer, too, if He chooses."

Bruce watched as his son waged a silent war with himself. An array of emotions flittered across his face. "I can't do this." In a huff, he turned on his heel and stormed off towards the far side of the lake away from the main house. Bruce let him go.

∽

Fueled by anger, Andrew stormed off to his truck and hit the gas. He had no real destination, he just needed to be as far from the ranch as possible. Away from any reminders of what a terrible loser he was. He saw the turnoff for the Dinosaur Valley State Park and took it. Even though the park closed at six p.m., there was no gate blocking the path. He kept driving until he reached the parking lot.

He took the familiar path to the same outcropping of rock he'd sought refuge at a few weeks earlier. Although darkness came early this time of year, it was still fairly clear, and with the full moon beaming, he could make out the Paluxy River Valley down below. Clearing his mind, he focused on the sounds of the river and the frogs and night owls in the surrounding forest. Sitting by himself, he began thinking about Melody's words once again. Only this time he was ready to listen. He'd had enough.

Reaching into his pocket, he retrieved the crumpled brochure she'd given him at the diner. It was too dark to make out most of the fine print, but the words, 'Fresh Start', stood out in big, bold letters at the top. Those two words resonated within him with a profoundness, and words from long ago filtered into his consciousness... *No one tears a piece of cloth from a new garment and puts it on an old garment; otherwise he will both tear the new, and the piece from the new will not match the old. And no one puts new wine into old wineskins; otherwise, the new wine will burst the skins, and it will be spilled out, and the skins will be ruined. But new wine must be put into fresh wineskins.*

Andrew wasn't sure what God was trying to tell him about garments and wineskins, but what he understood was this. If he was going to make a fresh start, it had to be a completely new one. He couldn't put a band-aid on the old wounds and expect them to heal. He finally understood that to heal he had to start anew. His heart quickened—he wanted to start now.

As quickly as he could in the moonlight, he scrambled down the path back to his truck. Using the interior light, he skimmed the brochure from front to back. He wasn't concerned with the history of the organization since Melody had already told him how it came about; he was more interested in their contact information. He found an 800 number at the bottom and dialed. It was an automated number that said the offices would be open Monday morning at eight a.m. and to leave a message.

Not wanting to leave a message, he was about to hang up in frustration when he heard the prompt for the schedule of meetings. He pressed #3 and listened as a recorded voice gave the dates, times, and venues of each meeting for the week. He'd missed all but one. There was one that night at eight p.m. He looked at the clock on his phone. It was seven-fifteen. If he hurried, he could just make it.

But, could he face going into the meeting alone? Melody had said she'd go with him if he wanted her to, but he had no way of getting a hold of her. He tossed the brochure down on the seat next to him in frustration. It fluttered to the seat, falling face down. He blinked. Her name and phone number, in capitals and red ink, jumped out at him. She must have written them on the back before she gave it to him. It had to be divine intervention. What else could it be?

"Thank you, Lord," he said quickly before he dialed her number. He prayed that she'd answer and that she wasn't busy. Somehow, he knew she wouldn't be.

"Hello?" He sighed in relief as he heard her tentative voice.

"Melody, it's Andrew. You know, from the diner."

"Is everything okay?"

"Yes and no," he answered honestly. "Um, there's a meeting tonight with Fresh Start at eight p.m. I was wondering if you would go with me?"

Andrew felt like it was a lifetime before he heard her say, "I'd be glad to. I can be ready in fifteen minutes."

True to her word, she was ready when he pulled up to her house fifteen minutes later. She gave him the directions to the meeting location and briefed him on what to expect. His palms oozed sweat as he gripped the steering wheel, and this time it had nothing to do with withdrawal symptoms.

"It's okay to be nervous."

"Does it show?" he asked.

"No, not really," she hedged.

She was attempting to lie for his benefit, but he appreciated the gesture. He pulled up to an unassuming brick stand-alone building. The sign said 'Pearson Technical Center'. Andrew looked over at Melody, his brows furrowed.

"It's a technical school during the day, but they rent out their classrooms in the evening," she said by way of explanation. After a beat, she asked, "Ready?"

He wasn't sure if he was or not, but he'd never know if he didn't try. He went back to the words he'd heard when he was on the rocks by the river. This wouldn't work if he wasn't ready to be made completely new. *Okay, Lord. I'm trusting that this is where You want me to be. I'm not exactly sure what I'm supposed to do other than show up. But I'm here. And I'm ready to be made new again.* Taking a deep, steadying breath, he opened the door. "Let's do this."

They walked in together. The classroom was of average size, and a circle of chairs filled the middle of the room. He gritted his teeth, realizing he wouldn't be able to hide in the back row. A few people recognized Melody, and she was greeted warmly. He wondered if she'd attended meetings with her mom, or maybe even her dad. Andrew would have to ask her about that later. Right now, he was just thankful that the spotlight was more on her than him. But he knew his time would come soon and that his anonymity was only fleeting.

Right at eight p.m., an older gentleman with salt and pepper hair walked into the room and greeted everyone. He asked them to take a seat around the circle. There were more chairs than there were people. Only about two-thirds were filled, which suited Andrew just fine. Melody sat next to him and patted his knee in reassurance.

"Good evening, everyone. Thank you for coming. My name

is Mark Waters, for those of you who don't know me. I'd like to go around the room and have each of you introduce yourself and say why you are here. It doesn't have to be your life story if you don't want it to be, just say as much as you're comfortable sharing." He started with a woman to his left and went counter-clockwise around the circle. Andrew was the seventh person in.

When it was his turn to stand and introduce himself, Melody gave his hand a gentle squeeze and whispered so no one else could hear, "You've got this."

It was just the encouragement he needed. He stood up, and with clarity in his voice said, "Hi. My name is Andrew McCarthy, and I'm an alcoholic and drug addict." Once the words left his lips, he felt the weight of the world lift from his shoulders. All of the burdens and shame he'd harbored for so long were set free as he finally admitted the truth. He told them about his mother, and how he'd turned to drink to deal with his guilt. The words just tumbled out.

The meeting lasted only an hour, and it seemed to Andrew that the time flew by. He'd learned so much in such a short time, but the biggest takeaway for him was that he wasn't alone in this. He had Melody, Mark, and the other members of the group supporting him. But most of all, he had the Lord supporting him in his transformation.

He felt cleansed and bolstered by the newfound feelings blossoming in him and he didn't want the night to end. As he was driving Melody home, he thanked her.

"For what?" she asked.

"For everything. For giving me a warm place to lay my head when I was drunk out of my mind. For being strong enough to tell me to my face what I needed to hear." He put the car in park as he pulled into her driveway and turned to face her. "For not giving up on me when I had given up on myself."

She beamed at him. "You're very welcome."

As she opened the door to get out, Andrew reached for her hand to stop her. She looked at him quizzically but stayed where she was. All of a sudden, he felt shy, his tongue felt thick, and it was difficult to swallow the lump in his throat.

"What is it, Andrew?"

"Would you…would you maybe like to have coffee with me sometime?" he managed to get out. "I mean, like not at the diner, but somewhere you don't actually work," he finished.

She chuckled. "I'd like that. I'd like that a lot." She smiled at him once more and then got out of the car and shut the door gently. He watched her walk all the way up to the door. Turning, she waved at him before she headed inside.

As he drove away, his heart felt lighter than it had in a long, long time.

CHAPTER 16

The weeks flew by. Thanksgiving passed without much fanfare. It was a rather somber gathering as Wendy had started her cancer treatment and was far too weak to join in the festivities much. Bruce still tried to make the best of the occasion and wheeled her into the family room for an hour or two at a time so she could be with the family even if she didn't feel up to visiting for long.

She also tried to FaceTime with her kids back home at least once a day, though sometimes Bruce had to finish the call because she was simply too exhausted. It was difficult for them to be so far away from their mother, but they were always encouraging and uplifting when they spoke to her. He also called them separately to let them know of any major updates on her treatment. In these conversations he was more direct with how she was actually faring. So far, there'd been no change in the tumor size. This sounded discouraging, but the doctors believed it was a good sign because it meant she wasn't getting worse.

Wendy was discouraged, but Bruce tried to help her see the bright side of things. It also helped that Natalie, Alyssa, and Elysha would be visiting them for a week at Christmas. Simon was staying in Australia to look after the house and farm, but he sent his mother handwritten notes and care packages almost every day. It was these little things that helped bolster her spirits. And Bruce also had a secret.

When Simon first mentioned that he'd need to stay in Sydney to look after things, Bruce had appreciated his wanting to handle the responsibilities back home, but when he'd seen how disappointed Wendy was, he couldn't let it go. He called Simon one night when she was asleep and talked to him about making arrangements so he could at least fly out for a few days to see his mother. Together, he and Simon worked out a plan with Colin and Ellis to handle things while he was gone. They didn't even tell Natalie and Adam their plans, wanting to keep the surprise as long as possible. So, Simon was flying out on the same day, but two hours later to avoid running into them at the airport.

Nate, Aiden, and even Andrew, had picked up the slack on the ranch, not allowing Bruce to help out at all. They had all decided he should spend all his time with Wendy and that they could handle everything having to do with the business. Bruce had been touched by their concern, even Andrew's. Although he was still scarce around the house, his mood seemed lighter, and the shadows under his eyes were gone. Nate had told Bruce that Andrew had begun to pitch in more, and not once in the last few weeks had he caught any hint of alcohol or drugs around him.

He still disappeared frequently at night, but he didn't come home too late and was never drunk. Bruce wondered where he went but didn't feel it was his place to question his son. He was a grown man and could make his own decisions. Besides, whatever choices he was making seemed to be having a positive impact on him, and Bruce didn't want to interrupt whatever transformation was happening. He just continued to pray for him at night as he did for Wendy.

It was the week after Thanksgiving when Bruce found out what or who was responsible for the transformation in Andrew. Bruce was restless and went out to the barn to see his horse, Gus. Wendy was resting, and Alyssa said she would look in on her while Bruce took some time for himself. He was feeding Gus an apple when he heard voices outside the barn door. One was distinctly female, but not one he recognized. As he was about to investigate, the doors opened and Andrew entered the barn with a young woman. They were holding hands and laughing.

Andrew stumbled as soon as he caught sight of him, immediately dropping the young woman's hand. "Oh, um…sorry, Dad. I didn't know anyone was in here." A faint flush crept up his neck.

So, this is why Andrew's been in a better mood of late. Not wanting to make a big deal about it, Bruce tried to appear as nonchalant as possible. "It's okay, son. I was just feeding ole' Gus here an apple. I like to sneak him a treat every now and then to let him know I haven't forgotten about him." He looked from Andrew to the woman, but neither said anything. The woman was staring at Andrew, and Andrew was looking everywhere but at his father.

Bruce didn't want to make things more awkward, so he decided to leave. "I was just headin' back to the house, anyway." He tipped his hat at the woman and then said to his son. "Have a good night, Andrew."

He couldn't exactly make out what was said, but harsh whispering sounded behind him, something that sounded like, 'Just talk to him, Andrew.'

"Dad..."

Bruce turned at his son's voice.

Andrew shuffled his feet a little before he continued. "I wanted to talk to you about something."

Bruce had no clue what Andrew wanted to talk about, but judging by his behavior, he sensed it was important. Preparing for the worst, he told himself that no matter what it was, he wouldn't judge. "Sure, son. What is it?"

"Um...I know you've noticed that I've been leaving in the evenings, and I wanted to tell you where I've been going." His voice was hesitant, and the dark-haired woman came to stand next to him and placed a reassuring hand on his shoulder. Something about her demeanor calmed Bruce.

Her voice was soft but direct. "I'm Melody. Andrew's ...friend."

"You're more than just my friend," Andrew said as he clasped her hand. Then he smiled at his dad. "She's my girlfriend, Dad."

Bruce's brows lifted. *Girlfriend?* "Congratulations, son. And it's a pleasure to meet you, Melody." Bruce's confusion must have shown on his face because Andrew continued to clarify.

"No, Dad, that wasn't what I wanted to tell you. I mean, I did want to tell you that, but that isn't all of it. I've been going to these meetings. AA meetings. Melody is the one who introduced me to the founder of Fresh Start and encouraged me to go. That's where I go in the evenings."

Bruce stared at Andrew as an array of emotions cascaded through him. How many times had he urged Andrew to get help, only to be brushed off? He'd prayed fervently that someone would get through to him, and finally, it seemed like his prayers had been answered. Overcome with joy and gratitude, he wrapped Andrew in a tight hug as tears rolled down his cheeks. "I love you, son." His voice was no more than a hoarse whisper.

It only took a moment before Andrew hugged him back. They embraced for a while before Bruce let him go and turned to Melody. He enveloped her in a giant hug, too, and whispered with tears still in his eyes, "Thank you. Thank you for reaching my son."

"You're welcome," she said, her own voice thick with emotion as she returned the hug.

Stepping back, Bruce wiped his eyes with the back of his hand and gave Andrew a watery grin. "I'm proud of you, son. And you know if there's anything I can do to support you, I will. You just let me know."

As he turned to leave, Andrew called out to him, "There is one thing, Dad."

"What's that?"

"I'd like to speak with Wendy, in private."

Bruce stared at his son for a long time. There was sincerity and uncertainty in his eyes, but he never looked away. "I'm sure she'd like that. In fact, she's had a pretty good day today. Why don't you come back to the house with me now? Melody, you can come too and visit with me while they talk."

"Thank you, Mr. McCarthy, but I have to be heading back now. I need to pick up my daughter from the babysitter."

"Another time, then."

They said their goodbyes and Bruce waited as Andrew walked her to her car. Both men were quiet as they strolled to the house together. Bruce went into the bedroom first while Andrew waited in the living room.

"Wendy?"

"Yes, darling." She was sitting up in bed with a crossword puzzle. She looked frail, but her eyes were bright, and there was some color in her cheeks.

Bruce sat on the bed next to her. "I don't know how to explain it, and I don't have time at the moment, but God is working amazing things in Andrew's life right now."

"That's wonderful, darling!" Her mouth curved into a smile as she squeezed his hand.

"He wants to talk to you…privately. Are you okay with that?"

Uncertainty flashed across her eyes. Bruce did his best to alleviate her fears. "I think this is a good thing. I feel the Lord is guiding him, honey."

"Then I won't hinder that. I'm feeling okay, so send him in."

"Oh Wendy. You're an amazing woman, and I love you with all my heart." He gazed into her eyes before placing a gentle kiss on her forehead. He then went out to get Andrew.

Andrew paced the floor as he waited for his father to come out of the bedroom. Wendy had been on his mind a lot, and he felt the Lord was leading him to speak with her. He needed to address the unresolved issues between them. There were so many things he wanted to say, but he didn't know where to start. He said a quick prayer that the Lord would give him wisdom and the right words to say to her.

When the bedroom door opened, he stopped pacing. His dad smiled and nodded at him, and Andrew felt both relief and apprehension rush through him. He'd been worried that Wendy wouldn't want to see him. Now he was worried about seeing her.

His dad must have read his fear because he put a hand on his shoulders. "She really wants to see you, Andrew. She's happy for you. We both are."

Unable to speak, Andrew could only nod. Taking a deep breath, he knocked gently on the door and then entered when he heard the soft reply. He didn't know what to expect, and the sight of Wendy wrapped in blankets and surrounded by pillows was difficult for him, especially with her broken leg sticking straight out from under the covers and propped on a pillow. She was thinner, not gaunt, but she definitely had lost weight, most likely from the chemo. It grieved Andrew's heart that she was going through this.

"Hello, Andrew. It's really nice to see you again."

Overcome with emotion, Andrew felt his eyes begin to water, and he began to shake.

"Oh, sweetheart. Don't cry. It's okay. Come here." She patted the space next to her.

He was almost undone with her compassion, but he found

himself hesitantly stepping forward and gingerly sitting next to her. She reached out her hand and squeezed his. He forced himself to look at her, tears unabashedly falling down his cheeks. "I'm so sorry."

"Hush now. You don't have anything to be sorry about."

"Yes, I do. I'm sorry that I've not been kind to you."

"But you've not been unkind, either."

Andrew shook his head. He didn't want her sympathy or for her to disregard his wrongdoings so easily. "No, I didn't try, and that was hurtful. I'm sorry for so many things." He took a breath before continuing. "I don't remember much that morning. I've wracked my brain for hours wondering if I was careless. I never meant to be. You have to know that," he implored.

"I know that."

"I'm sorry you got hurt. I didn't want that. I don't want you to be in pain. But most of all, I'm sorry I never gave you a chance. I can see how happy you make my dad, and now…" His voice broke.

"Shhh…we don't know anything yet. The Lord knows my last breath. Your dad and I have accepted that. And my last breath isn't today. So let's not think about tomorrow. I want to live for today. And today is a new beginning for you and me. I love your father very much…and I love you, too. I hope that one day you'll truly believe that."

Although his heart felt heavy, he smiled through his tears. Her acceptance and love were almost more than he could handle. He returned the squeeze of her hand. "I think I already do."

They talked a bit longer, but Wendy began slurring her words. She was tired. He thanked her for giving him time and for forgiving him. They hugged each other, and when he left, his heart felt lighter. He sincerely hoped that God would give her more time. More time so he could get to know her better, but also more time with his dad, because he deserved as much happiness as he could get.

CHAPTER 17

The days passed quickly as Wendy progressed with the treatments. There still had been no change, which the doctors continued to assure them was a good sign, but it was hard to find comfort in no change. It also frustrated Bruce when the doctor called Wendy back into the hospital to redo bloodwork and the CT scan they'd only done the week before.

"Why do we need to go back again?" He couldn't hide the frustration in his voice when he was on the phone with Dr. Walters.

"I understand your annoyance, Bruce, and I sincerely apologize. The test results and imaging weren't conclusive, and I want to run them again."

"Is this something I should be worried about? The last time you wanted to rerun some things, it didn't bode well for us."

"I promise it's nothing like that. I'd tell you if it was."

Somewhat mollified, Bruce agreed to bring Wendy back. It

was only four days before Christmas, and the round trip to Dallas was a long one and always took a lot out of her. Bruce wanted to ensure she had enough time to recover before her family flew in on the twenty-third. The trip was uneventful, and the doctor made sure they were in and out as quickly as possible. He told them he should have the test results back in a couple of days, and he would call.

The morning of the twenty-third, Bruce was like a kid in a candy store. He couldn't wait for six p.m. to get there. Natalie had texted him late the previous evening that they were on their way. He'd arranged for a car service to pick them up from the airport and drive them to the ranch. Then Simon had texted him a couple hours later to say he was on his way as well.

"What has gotten into you, darling? You haven't been able to sit still all morning. Are you really that anxious for Natalie and Adam to get here?" Wendy asked.

"Yes, I am, my darling." He grinned at her. It wasn't a lie. He was excited for them to get here, but he was also excited to surprise them all with Simon's arrival. Finally, a car pulled in the drive and he hollered that they were here. He carefully helped Wendy off the couch and walked with her to greet everyone on the front porch.

Natalie was the first to jump out of the Yukon and was up the porch steps and in her mother's arms in a matter of seconds. Adam wasn't far behind with baby Elysha. Bruce knew he'd made the right decision to fly them out when he saw the look of pure joy on his wife's face. All these weeks she'd been so resilient as she went through all the tests and treatments, and it felt good to do something nice for her. He also couldn't wait to see the look on all their faces when Simon showed up.

Everyone sat around the family room and chatted while Bruce finished preparing dinner with Alyssa's help. Aiden would be by the following day for Christmas Eve dinner, and he was bringing his girlfriend, Kimberly. Andrew was out with the cattle and would hopefully be by after dinner. If it was too late, they'd see him at the Christmas Eve dinner. He was also bringing Melody, so they were going to have a full house this holiday. Bruce was excited to bring both families together under one roof.

Dinner was about ready and Bruce kept checking his phone. Nate had texted him periodically, once to let him know when Simon arrived and again when they left the airport. He was supposed to text when they'd reached the outskirts of town.

"Why do you keep checking your phone?" Wendy asked. "You haven't put it down for the last hour."

Bruce swallowed hard. "Oh, I was just checking on Nate. He said to go ahead and start dinner without him. He'll be a little late."

"We can make sure to keep a plate warm for him when he comes home," Wendy said.

Bruce smiled. That was his Wendy, always thinking of others. They gathered around the dinner table, and Bruce gave thanks. They tucked into the spread of roasted chicken and dumplings, green bean casserole, scalloped potatoes, and homemade rolls. Just as everyone had been served and was digging into their food, a truck pulled up.

"That must be Nate!" Bruce said as he jumped up from the table.

"Well, I'm sure he knows the way, dear." Wendy looked at him with scrunched brows. Bruce could only grin like a fool. Wendy's gaze shifted between him and the door and back at the others at the table. "What's going on?"

No one knew, and all eyes were on the door when Bruce opened it for Nate. He stepped through the door with a big grin that matched his father's. "Hi, everyone. I found something that may belong to you."

He stepped aside, and Simon walked through the door. There was a chorus of cheers and laughter as everyone shouted their surprise and glee at his arrival. Bruce helped Wendy up from the table so she could hug her son. Tears flowed freely down her cheeks as she held him. Bruce's eyes teared up, too, at the joyous reunion.

"Simon! I can't believe you're here!" Wendy cried as she hugged him.

"It was Bruce's idea. He called and convinced me to come."

"Who's watching the farm?"

"Colin and Ellis are pitching in. I'm only here for a few days. I fly back out the day after Christmas, but I really wanted to see you."

"I'll take whatever time I have with you." She smiled at her son and then looked over her shoulder at Bruce. "Thank you. From the bottom of my heart, thank you."

Bruce enveloped both of them in a giant hug. "Anything for you, my love."

Dinner was a family affair; long after they finished eating, they sat around the table, talking, laughing and sharing stories.

Eventually, Wendy's eyes began to droop, and Bruce knew it was time to wind the evening down. There would be plenty of time to talk and fellowship the next day when everyone would be there.

⁓

The following morning, everyone slept in. Long days of travel, jet lag, and the excitement of the previous evening had taken its toll. They all enjoyed a late breakfast, and that afternoon, Bruce suggested Nate take Natalie and Adam out on the ranch for a hayride. That gave Wendy some time to rest before Aiden and Kimberly and Andrew and Melody arrived for Christmas Eve dinner.

At about four p.m., Bruce was about to wake Wendy when his cell phone rang. His face dropped when he saw the number. It was Dr. Walters.

"Who is it, darling?"

"It's Dr. Walters." He watched as her face mirrored his.

"Well, go ahead and answer it. We'll face whatever it is together."

Nodding, he sat beside her and held her hand while he answered the phone. "Hello."

"Hello, Bruce? It's Dr. Walters."

Bruce put the call on speakerphone and set the cell phone on the bed between him and Wendy. "Hello, Dr. Walters. You're on speakerphone. Wendy is here. We weren't expecting your call on Christmas Eve."

"I know. And I'm sorry to bother you on Christmas Eve, but this couldn't wait."

Bruce looked at Wendy with anguish in his heart. "How bad is it?" he asked.

"It's not."

"Excuse me?" Bruce cocked one brow at Wendy, seeking assurance from her that he'd heard the doctor correctly. She looked just as confused as he felt.

"That's just it. It's not bad at all. In fact, it's the complete opposite of bad."

"Okay, doc, you're going to have to give it to us straight because we aren't following ya."

"It's gone. The cancer is gone."

"What do you mean, gone? Like, shrunk?"

"No, I mean gone. Gone. As in we can't find a trace of it. That's why I had you bring Wendy back for more tests. I didn't believe it the first time, so I reran the tests and scans. I've never seen anything like it in all my years." Dr. Walters voice was filled with wonder.

"I can't believe it!" Wendy cried.

Bruce wrapped her in his arms and they cried together. "Praise the Lord!"

"It is a miracle," Dr. Walters said. "There are no documented cases, at least not that I can find, of a glioblastoma tumor vanishing. Wendy, we'll still want you to come again in a few weeks to make sure, and we'll monitor you for at least a year after that. But there's no reason to think you won't live a long and cancer free life."

After thanking the doctor, Bruce hung up the phone, and for a minute, all they could do was stare at each other open-mouthed.

"God is good," he said as he reached for Wendy's hand.

"He is. I can't wait to tell the kids."

"Let's tell them at dinner when everyone is here," he suggested.

"That's a wonderful idea!" Wendy's smile melted his heart. He pulled her close and kissed the top of her head, breathing in the smell of her freshly washed hair. He wasn't going to lose her. Praise God! Relief washed through him as he held her tight.

~

LATER THAT EVENING, as they all sat around the dinner table, Bruce stood up to get everyone's attention. However, he was interrupted by Andrew.

"Dad, I have something I want to announce."

Bruce looked about to burst, but Wendy just laughed as she tapped his hand. "It's okay, darling. Let Andrew go first."

"And after Andrew, I have something to say, too," Aiden followed with a grin.

"We do, too," Natalie and Adam chimed in as they held hands and giggled like children.

Chuckling, Bruce glanced at Wendy and shook his head. "Okay, then, why don't we go around the table, starting with Andrew, and Wendy and I will bring up the rear."

Everyone nodded in agreement and then all eyes turned to Andrew. He cleared his throat before speaking. "All of you know that I've struggled with alcohol and drugs over the years. I used them to hide the pain and the guilt I felt from Mom's death. But Christmas is a time of new beginnings, and I want to celebrate the birth of Christ with a birth of my own, or actually, a re-birth." Pausing, he took a slow breath before continuing. "I've rededicated my life to Christ, and I'm proud to announce that I've been clean and sober for two months now."

Wendy squeezed Bruce's hand and fought tears of joy as applause and congratulations circled around the table. "That's wonderful news, son. We're all so proud of you," Bruce said.

"Well, speaking of new births," Natalie began. "We have one of our own to share." All eyes were on her now. "Adam and I are expecting!"

"What?" Wendy was the first to exclaim. Her eyes widened with disbelief. Natalie had tears in her eyes and nodded at her mum. "Mmm-hmmm. I'm twelve weeks! We didn't want to say anything until I was this far along because we weren't sure if it was viable. But we've heard the heartbeat, and our child is healthy and strong. Elysha's going to be a big sister!"

Wendy burst into tears as another chorus of congratulations moved through the group. Reaching out, she hugged her daughter and whispered in her ear, "That's the best news, sweetheart. Congratulations!"

Once the fanfare died down, everyone turned to Aiden.

"Okay, so I don't have a birth of any sort to announce…at least not yet. But I do have a new beginning to announce." He glanced at Kimberly with a broad smile. "I've asked Kimberly to be my wife, and she's accepted."

For a third time that night, there was a round of congratulations, and they all raised their glasses to toast Kimberly into the family. It was hard to imagine that things could get any better, but Wendy and Bruce hadn't shared their news yet. News she was still coming to terms with herself. It was so amazing.

Rising from his seat, Bruce stood beside her and placed his hand on her shoulder. She reached up and squeezed his.

He cleared his throat and everyone grew silent. Wendy's heart beat loudly as she waited for him to share their news. "Words cannot express how truly blessed we feel this holiday. Not just having all our family members under one roof, but to know that our family is expanding with new life." He glanced at Natalie and Adam. "New members." His gaze shifted to Kimberly. "And new beginnings." He then nodded at Andrew. "But, we're also blessed with a Christmas miracle. My wife and your mother will be around to experience all of these new beginnings for many years to come."

Stunned silence filled the room as Bruce's words sunk in. Then everyone talked at once.

"What do you mean?"

"The cancer is gone?"

"How?"

"When did you find out?"

Bruce held up his hand. "There'll be plenty of time to answer those questions today, tomorrow, and many, many months from now. We don't know the specifics, other than God is an amazing healer. Wendy's doctor called to tell us there's no sign of the cancer at all. She will have to continue being monitored to make sure it doesn't come back, but we have faith that it won't."

One at a time her family hugged her. Natalie, Adam, Elysha, Simon, Nate, Alyssa, the children, Aiden, Kimberly, Andrew and Melody. And then Bruce. It was a dream come true. A prayer answered. God was so good and she and Bruce were so blessed to be surrounded by such a loving family. And best of all, God willing, she'd be here to share their joys for years to come.

~

CHRISTMAS MORNING, as they all gathered around the tree and Bruce distributed the gifts, Wendy's eyes flooded with tears as she opened her gift from Natalie. Earlier that year, when Natalie was wondering what she would do to fill her time after temporarily losing custody of Elysha, she'd hinted she might write a book, and here it was! *We'll Never Forget You...* It was Paige's story, and her beautiful, cheeky face filled the paperback cover. Wendy couldn't believe it! She turned to Natalie and hugged her. "This is a wonderful gift, Natalie. Thank you so much! I can't wait to read it."

Paige might not have been there in body, but her spirit lived on amongst them. Not only in the pages of the book, but in her precious daughter, Elysha, who looked at Wendy and then pointed to the book. "Mumma."

EPILOGUE

Twelve Months Later

Turning around, Wendy fought tears as the organist began playing the wedding processional. Bruce was flanked by Kimberly on his left, and Melody on his right. He'd been so honored when separately they'd asked him to walk them down the aisle. So many good things had happened over the previous twelve months, and this was the culminating moment.

Natalie had given birth to a healthy baby boy, and she and Adam had named him Caleb Gregory. Elysha had taken her responsibility as big sister in her stride and loved him to bits. With help from Ellis, Simon had started his shelter at the farm for troubled youth, and with Melody's help, Andrew had stayed sober and never looked back. Now he was a young man with pride and purpose, forgiven and free of his demons. And he loved Jasmine, Melody's daughter, as if she were his own.

She'd looked so adorable as she walked down the aisle carrying a basket of flowers ahead of the bridesmaids.

But best of all, Wendy had been given a clean bill of health. Her cancer had stayed away, and she and Bruce could now plan a long and happy life together surrounded by their families.

After Bruce kissed his about-to-be daughters-in-law and shook hands with his sons, he returned to sit beside Wendy. Taking her hand, he squeezed it and warmth spread though her. How she loved this man. After so much heart-ache, God had blessed them beyond measure, and she knew that no matter what, their love would last the distance.

You turned my wailing into dancing;
You removed my sackcloth and clothed me with joy,
that my heart may sing Your praises and not be silent.
Lord my God, I will praise You forever.

A NOTE FROM THE AUTHOR

I hope you enjoyed "A Time to Rejoice"! I felt like I was losing good friends when I typed "The End!" Bruce and Wendy and their families have all come to mean so much to me, but all good things have to come to an end at some stage. I'm glad it all worked out for them lol!

Anyway, get set for a brand new series! Something a little different, but nevertheless, still God-honoring and uplifting.

"Her Kind-Hearted Billionaire" is Book 1 in *The Billionaires with Heart Christian Romance Series,* and is now available to order. It will be free to read on Kindle Unlimited. You can read the first chapter at the end of this note.

To make sure you don't miss it, and to be notified of all my new releases, why not join my Readers' list? You'll also receive a free thank-you copy of "Hank and Sarah - A Love Story", a clean love story with God at the center.

Enjoyed "A Time to Rejoice"? You can make a big difference. Help other people find this book by writing a review and telling them why you liked it. Honest reviews of my books help bring them to the attention of other readers just like yourself, and I'd be very grateful if you could spare just five minutes to leave a review (it can be as short as you like) on the book's Amazon page.

Oh, and don't forget to keep reading for a bonus chapter of "Her Kind-Hearted Billionaire". I think you'll enjoy it.

Blessings,
Juliette

Her Kind-Hearted Billionaire

Chapter 1

Sydney, Australia

Nicholas Barrington sat behind his desk on the forty-first floor of the towers bearing his family's name and removed his pre-prepared meal from his lunch bag. Below, Sydney Harbour shimmered in the midday sun and looked spectacular. A small tugboat, looking much like a toy from this height, guided a large cruise ship through the harbour towards the heads, while a number of yachts sliced through the water easily in what Nick assumed was a strong breeze, given the trim of their sails. The problem was, being on the forty-first floor, he was removed from reality. The view was sensational, but he felt like a spectator. He'd much rather be a participant.

A firm knock sounded on his office door, pulling his gaze from the vista. Nicholas swivelled around. Alden, his brother and fellow director, sauntered in and sunk into the chair on the opposite side of the desk. "Taking time for lunch today, bro?" At thirty-one, Alden was two years younger than Nicholas and had the same sea-blue eyes, although his hair was much darker.

"Yes. I was just about to eat. Did you bring yours?" For a moment, Nicholas forgot he was talking with his brother. Of course Alden hadn't brought it.

Alden scoffed, eyeing Nicholas's bag with amusement. "It'll be here in five minutes."

Nicholas pulled out his sandwich and salad, glad he didn't have to wait for his to be delivered.

"Eating in here today?" Charity, their younger sister, appeared in the doorway. The sharp bob framing her pixie-like face was the same dark colour as Alden's, but she had their late mother's emerald green eyes. She plopped onto the chair next to Alden and pulled a portable blender filled with green powder from her carry bag. Opening a bottle of water, she poured half of it in and hit the button.

"That looks disgusting," Nicholas shouted over the whir of the machine.

"Try some if you like."

He quickly shook his head. "No thanks. I'll stick to my sandwich."

Moments later, a young man knocked tentatively on the door holding a rectangular food box. Alden waved him in and took the box from him.

Setting it on the desk, he peeled back the cardboard lid, revealing a large steak with new potatoes and green beans. Although it smelled appetising, as Nicholas took the last bite of his sandwich and moved onto the salad, he was thankful his tastes weren't the same as his siblings. He was a simple man with simple tastes.

"It's all right, but it could be better," Alden commented after swallowing his first mouthful.

Nicholas ignored his brother's comment and instead focused on Charity who'd just turned the blender off. The silence was very welcome.

"So, you know I was meant to be flying to Bali tomorrow for that meditation retreat?" She tilted her head and glanced at him as she poured some of the green concoction into a glass.

He nodded. Charity had been delving into meditation and something about self-praise and how to be her own deity of late. Not what Nicholas would have considered a worthwhile venture, but, each to his own. He'd started exploring things of a spiritual nature as well, but his initial explorations had led him to a traditional church, although he hadn't totally made up his mind about whether it was worth it or not as yet.

"Looks like I'll have to postpone it to another day." She released a frustrated sigh before taking a mouthful of the disgusting looking green concoction.

"Why's that?"

"Why?" Charity's green eyes bulged. "Because of that lazy pilot." Her voice rose to a crescendo and Nicholas wouldn't have been surprised if the whole floor had heard.

"Ugh, don't even get me started." Alden shook his head, waving a fork in the air.

Charity leaned forward. "Can you believe he told me he can't work tomorrow? I mean, I'm his boss. It's not like we're ordering him to fly every day. He gets plenty of time off. I just needed him for one day."

"Why can't he take you?" Nicholas asked in a calm voice.

"His daughter's having surgery. I get that family is important and all that, but honestly, it's only a few hours each way. He'd be back before she even woke up."

Nicholas studied his sister with sadness. He doubted she knew that Roger's small daughter had been born with special needs and her surgeries required extensive preparation. Even the anesthesia was a risk. But it was no use saying anything. She wouldn't understand or care. "Did he suggest anyone else who could step in?"

"I don't want anyone else. They wouldn't know our plane like he does." Charity blew out another breath and sipped her concoction. "Anyway, I think we should fire him and look for someone else." Shifting in her chair, she crossed her long, slim legs and adjusted her skirt.

"I agree." Alden said. "Last time he took me to Dubai, we were an hour late. He said it was because they didn't have a place for us to land, but isn't it his job to make sure all of that's prepared ahead of time?"

Nicholas sighed. "That's hardly his fault. Sometimes unexpected things happen that are out of anyone's control. You know Roger's competent and he always does his best."

"You're so naive, big brother. You always want to see the good in everybody. No wonder they take advantage of you." Alden gave him a withering look.

Nicholas pursed his lips. He wished his siblings could show a little more humility and understanding, especially since they'd been given everything they had. How could they be so cruel and selfish when it came to others?

Taking a sip from his water bottle, Nicholas shut out his

siblings as they continued talking about things he couldn't relate to. Although the three of them were very different, it saddened him that they weren't closer. Without any other family, they only had each other. But all they ever talked about was the business and what gave them pleasure, like Charity's Bali trip. Beyond that, very little of depth ever entered their conversations. While the two continued to talk about things of no interest to him, Nicholas returned to his work, but his ears pricked up when Alden mentioned their late grandfather, James Barrington.

"You know, old James wouldn't have liked us wasting the money on a lousy staffer. Just because a man's nice enough doesn't make him worth the money." It seemed they'd returned to the issue of whether to fire Roger or not and Nicholas groaned. From what he remembered of James Barrington, firing a man because of an important family issue would have been the last thing he would have done.

When he died, the three siblings had inherited their grandfather's fortune which he'd amassed during the mining boom of the eighties. A billion for each, plus the company divided between them. Now the trio lacked for nothing, but as much as Nicholas appreciated the life he now had, he would much have preferred his grandfather, and his parents, to still be alive. How different things would have been if they'd inherited instead of the three grandkids.

He sighed sadly. Yes, he'd give just about anything to have his parents back. It didn't seem fair that their lives had been snuffed out while they were still in their prime.

"So, do you think we should fire him? After he takes me to

Bali, of course?" Charity asked nonchalantly, inspecting her perfectly manicured nails.

"Don't be a fool," Alden said harshly.

For a moment, Nicholas held hopes that his brother might stick up for the man, but they were soon dashed when Alden continued. "You should probably wait until he brings you back from Bali. You don't want to be stuck there!" He laughed, and Charity joined in.

Nicholas seethed. He had to say something, but he needed to remain calm and rational. An emotional defense of the pilot wouldn't go over well with his siblings. "Why don't we give him another chance? His daughter is having surgery, it's hardly a time to be selfish."

Charity huffed with exasperation. "Whatever you say, big brother. Although I don't see how it affects you, since you never use the private jet anyway." Her voice dripped with sarcasm.

Biting his lip, Nicholas brushed her comments and attitude off. They'd soon forget about the pilot and move on to a discussion about shoes or something as equally trivial.

"Well, I'm headed out. I've got a hot yoga class this afternoon." Charity stood, tossed her rubbish in the bin, and then picked her blender up.

"Don't you need more than that shake before working out?" Alden waved the last piece of steak on his fork as if he were teasing her with it.

She rolled her eyes. "Keep your cow, thanks." With that, she turned and left the room, teetering on her stilettos.

Alden mopped up the last of his gravy, said a brief goodbye to Nicholas, and then also left the office.

Leaning back in his chair, Nicholas released a slow breath and gazed out the window. The cruise ship was long gone, but a Manly ferry was approaching Circular Quay, leaving white frothy water in its wake.

As much as he loved his siblings, he also loved his peace and quiet. He sometimes wondered about their grandfather and whether he'd be pleased with how his grandchildren were handling his fortune. James Barrington was renown for his kindness, a rarity in the ruthless mining industry, and Nicholas wished he'd gotten to know him better before he passed. He sensed he could have learned a lot from him, and not just about the business. He'd heard that James Barrington was a religious man. Another rarity in the industry.

Swivelling his chair all the way around, Nicholas set back to work, tapping his fingers on his keyboard, opening emails from clients, studying spreadsheets. Millions of dollars in transactions and exchanges occurred on a weekly basis and the company was doing well, but as Managing Director, he needed to stay on top of it.

Their clients were happy, and he had reason to be proud of the company that he and his siblings had maintained and grown since taking over almost ten years ago. To the world at large, they were a success.

But sometimes, in the still of night when he had time to think, he wondered was what success really was. What was he missing by spending all his days on the forty-first floor?

Grab your copy of Her Kind-Hearted Billionaire.

OTHER BOOKS BY JULIETTE DUNCAN

Find all of Juliette Duncan's books on her website:
www.julietteduncan.com/library

∽

Billionaires with Heart Christian Romance Series

Her Kind-Hearted Billionaire

A reluctant billionaire, a grieving young woman, and the trip that changes their lives forever...

Her Generous Billionaire

A grieving billionaire, a solo mother, and a woman determined to sabotage their relationship...

Her Disgraced Billionaire

A messed up billionaire who lands in jail, a nurse who throws a challenge he can't refuse...

"The Billionaires with Heart Christian Romance Series" is a series of stand-alone books that are both God honoring and entertaining. Get your copy now,

enjoy and be blessed!

The True Love Series

Set in Australia, what starts out as simple love story grows into a family saga, including a dad battling bouts of depression and guilt, an ex-wife with issues of her own, and a young step-mum trying to mother a teenager who's confused and hurting. Through it all, a love story is woven. A love story between a caring God and His precious children as He gently draws them to Himself and walks with them through the trials and joys of life.

"A beautiful Christian story. I enjoyed all of the books in this series. They all brought out Christian concepts of faith in action."

"Wonderful set of books. Weaving the books from story to story. Family living, God, & learning to trust Him with all their hearts."

The Precious Love Series

The Precious Love Series continues the story of Ben, Tessa and Jayden from the The True Love Series, although each book can be read on its own. All of the books in this series will warm your heart and draw you closer to the God who loves and cherishes you without condition.

"I loved all the books by Juliette, but those about Jaydon and Angie's stories are my favorites...can't wait for the next one..."

"Juliette Duncan has earned my highest respect as a Christian romance writer. She continues to write such touching stories about real life and the tragedies, turmoils, and joys that happen while we are living. The words that she uses to write about her characters relationships with God can only come from someone that has had a very close & special with her Lord and Savior herself. I have read all of her books and if you are a reader of Christian fiction books I would highly recommend her books." Vicki

The Shadows Series

An inspirational romance, a story of passion and love, and of God's inexplicable desire to free people from pasts that haunt them so they can live a life full of His peace, love and forgiveness, regardless of the circumstances.

Book 1, *"Lingering Shadows"* is set in England, and follows the story of Lizzy, a headstrong, impulsive young lady from a privileged background, and Daniel, a roguish Irishman who sweeps her off her feet. But can Lizzy leave the shadows of her past behind and give Daniel the love he deserves, and will Daniel find freedom and release in God?

∽

Hank and Sarah - A Love Story, *the Prequel to "The Madeleine Richards Series" is a FREE thank you gift for joining my mailing list. You'll also be the first to hear about my next books and get exclusive sneak previews. Get your free copy at*
www.julietteduncan.com/subscribe

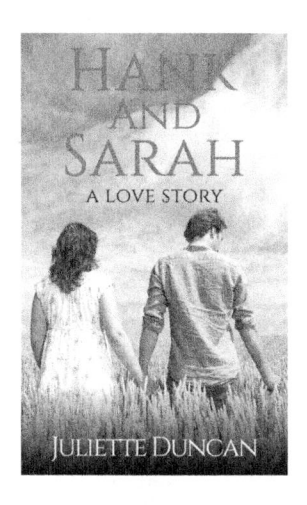

The Madeleine Richards Series

Although the 3 book series is intended mainly for pre-teen/ Middle Grade girls, it's been read and enjoyed by people of all ages.

"Juliette has a fabulous way of bringing her characters to life. Maddy is at typical teenager with authentic views and actions that truly make it feel like you are feeling her pain and angst. You want to enter into her situation and make everything better. Mom and soon to be dad respond to her with love and gentle persuasion while maintaining their faith and trust in Jesus, whom they know, will give them wisdom as they continue on their lives journey. Appropriate for teenage readers but any age can enjoy." Amazon Reader

∾

The Potter's House Books...stories of hope, redemption, and second chances. Find out more here:

http://pottershousebooks.com/our-books/

The Homecoming

Kayla McCormack is a famous pop-star, but her life is a mess. Dane Carmichael has a disability, but he has a heart for God. He had a crush on her at school, but she doesn't remember him. His simple faith and life fascinate her, But can she surrender her life of fame and fortune to find true love?

Unchained

Imprisoned by greed – redeemed by love

Sally Richardson has it all. A devout, hard-working, well-respected husband, two great kids, a beautiful home, wonderful friends. Her life is perfect. Until it isn't.

When Brad Richardson, accountant, business owner, and respected church member, is sentenced to five years in jail, Sally is shell-shocked. How had she not known about her husband's fraudulent activity? And how, as an upstanding member of their tight-knit community, did he ever think he'd get away with it? He's defrauded clients, friends, and fellow church members. She doubts she can ever trust him again.

Locked up with murderers and armed robbers, Brad knows that the only way to survive his incarceration is to seek God with all his heart - something he should have done years ago. But how does he convince his family that his remorse is genuine? Will they ever forgive him?

He's failed them. But most of all, he's failed God. His poor decisions have ruined this once perfect family.

They've lost everything they once held dear. Will they lose each other as well?

∽

Blessings of Love

She's going on mission to help others. He's going to win her heart.

Skye Matthews, bright, bubbly and a committed social work major, is the pastor's daughter. She's in love with Scott Anderson, the most eligible bachelor, not just at church, but in the entire town.

Scott lavishes her with flowers and jewellery and treats her like a lady, and Skye has no doubt that life with him would be amazing. And yet, sometimes, she can't help but feel he isn't committed enough. Not to her, but to God.

She knows how important Scott's work is to him, but she has a niggling feeling that he isn't prioritising his faith, and that concerns her. If only he'd join her on the mission trip to Burkina Faso...

Scott Anderson, a smart, handsome civil engineering graduate, has just received the promotion he's been working for for months. At age twenty-four, he's the youngest employee to ever hold a position of this calibre, and he's pumped.

Scott has been dating Skye long enough to know that she's 'the one', but just when he's about to propose, she asks him to go on mission with her. His plans of marrying her are thrown to the wind.

Can he jeopardise his career to go somewhere he's never heard of, to work amongst people he'd normally ignore?

If it's the only way to get a ring on Skye's finger, he might just risk it...

And can Skye's faith last the distance when she's confronted with a truth she never expected?

~

Stand Alone Christian Romantic Suspense

Leave Before He Kills You

When his face grew angry, I knew he could murder…

That face drove me and my three young daughters to flee across Australia.

I doubted he'd ever touch the girls, but if I wanted to live and see them grow, I had to do something.

The plan my friend had proposed was daring and bold, but it also gave me hope.

My heart thumped. What if he followed?

Radical, honest and real, this Christian romantic suspense is one woman's journey to freedom you won't put down…get your copy and read it now.

ABOUT THE AUTHOR

Juliette Duncan is a Christian fiction author, passionate about writing stories that will touch her readers' hearts and make a difference in their lives. Although a trained school teacher, Juliette spent many years working alongside her husband in their own business, but is now relishing the opportunity to follow her passion for writing stories she herself would love to read. Based in Brisbane, Australia, Juliette and her husband have five adult children, eight grandchildren, and an elderly long haired dachshund. Apart from writing, Juliette loves exploring the great world we live in, and has travelled extensively, both within Australia and overseas. She also enjoys social dancing and eating out.

Connect with Juliette:

Email: juliette@julietteduncan.com

Website: www.julietteduncan.com

Facebook: www.facebook.com/JulietteDuncanAuthor

Twitter: https://twitter.com/Juliette_Duncan

Printed in Great Britain
by Amazon